Blood Red Star

Cort Keller and his gang are on the run after a successful robbery, but a posse led by Marshal Nate Whitman, aided by his Crow Indian friend Little Hawk, are closing in on them. Cort goes to the house of his cousin Coy Brandon, ex-outlaw turned family man, for help. But when Coy is gunned down, and the Keller gang starts to fall apart, Cort is forced to reconsider his way of life if he is to survive.

By the same author

Showdown in Badlands

Blood Red Star

Shorty Gunn

A Black Horse Western

ROBERT HALE

© Shorty Gunn 2017
First published in Great Britain 2017

ISBN 978-0-7198-2196-7

The Crowood Press
The Stable Block
Crowood Lane
Ramsbury
Marlborough
Wiltshire SN8 2HR

www.bhwesterns.com

Robert Hale is an imprint
of The Crowood Press

Printed and bound in Great Britain by
CPI Group (UK) Ltd, Croydon, CR0 4YY

CHAPTER ONE

The narrow cliff-side trail was barely visible under the fading glow of moon-down as the first promise of dawn began coloring the eastern horizon behind stony peaks. The noisy clattering of horses' hoofs revealed shadowed images of four riders reaching the rim trail all but lost behind a thin screen of scraggy junipers, clinging precariously to the steep drop-off. The men pushed their horses and themselves double hard all night fighting through thick brush and downed pines until the lead rider, Cort Keller, reined to a stop at the trail head. Twisting in the saddle, he talked low and fast.

'Red, you stay here and watch our back trail for at least an hour. I think we lost that posse in the dark, but you never know for sure. Even Nate Whitman can't track at night. Neither can that Indian kid who rides with him. If you see any lantern light coming, get kicking and follow us fast to Janesville. We'll head for Bluestone ranch to get fresh horses at Coy's if we have to. If you don't bring bad news, we can stay there and rest a few days before moving on.'

'Why me?' Red, whose bible name was Rodney and something he hated, barked back. 'That'll just leave me stuck here like fish bait while you three make tracks!'

'Just do it. I don't have time to argue about it now. We'll

be at Coy's by late afternoon. Either way you won't be more than an hour behind us. I hope you bring good news when you catch up.'

The three riders led by Cort Keller, cousin Wic Casner and gang member Tyge Fan, started their horses down the dangerous trail while Red sat in the saddle muttering to himself watching them ride past.

'Good luck, Red,' Wic called out.

Fan, last in line, decided to needle Red as was his usual habit. He liked agitating Red's short fuse temper. 'You keep a sharp eye out, Red. We don't want Whitman to get any closer to us than he was back in New Hope, all right?'

'If you're so dang worried about it, why don't you stay here and watch for him your own self!'

'I can't. Your brother said that's your job and he's the boss, ain't he?'

Red didn't answer this time. Cort was the leader for sure, even if he was his younger brother. He always carefully planned the robberies insisting no one get killed unless there was no choice and some fool decided to be a hero going for a gun. When the sound of horses' hoofs on slab rock faded away, Red eased out of the saddle and climbed a rocky outcrop nearby that gave him an expansive view of rolling hill country that the gang had spent most of the night fighting their way through. He sat trying to get comfortable gazing back at the still murky image of endless cross-cut canyons cloaked in brushy cedars and jack pines. Cort had to be right. No one could track even four riders through those tangles in the dark. The more time he spent staring at it, the more he became convinced they had to be in the clear. Nothing showed. No bird sang. Only the sound of a waking coyote howling far-off broke the eerie silence. Red relaxed, rubbing the tiredness out of his eyes. The pocket watch ticking loudly in his vest seemed to make the minutes drag by even slower. He sat and stared until he'd had enough. It had to be close to an hour by now. He stood, stretching out the kinks, anxious to leave, taking one more long look before saddling up.

Suddenly, right at the limit of vision, he thought he saw the tiniest flicker of distant lantern light. It blinked on then off for several seconds as his heart skipped a beat of fear. Maybe his eyes were playing tricks on him. He squinted harder, holding his breath. There it was again, this time a bit clearer. The posse was somehow still following them, night or not. Nate Whitman, the United States Marshal out of New Hope, was true to his reputation as a dogged tracker who never gave up. The Keller gang had robbed a US Mail coach the previous day of twelve hundred dollars in payroll money for cavalry troops stationed at Indian Wells. Not only had they been successful, but this time done so robbing a government carrier. That meant not only was Nate Whitman determined to run them down, but also federal authorities might use horse soldiers to pursue them. If caught, they'd all rot in federal prison for twenty years. Red watched the dancing lanterns only a minute longer. He'd seen all he needed or wanted to. Abandoning his rocky perch he climbed into the saddle, urging his horse down the slippery cliff trail. He had to catch up to Cort fast to tell him they were all still in big trouble, whether he liked it or not.

Where the trail bottomed out, it wound through scattered pines and willows angling farther east. Sometimes it was as easy to follow a game trail, used by wandering elk and mule deer. At others, it led across hard slab rock showing almost no sign at all. Keller and the rest of his men had used this escape route before traveling west to hide out at scattered ranches of friends. He let his horse out at a steady, ground-eating gallop dodging sharp pine snags, with Wic and Fan

7

right behind him. His mind was still on Red, wondering what he'd seen. Was Whitman still on their trail, or had they shaken him in their wild ride through the night. He wouldn't shake that question until Red caught up to tell them if they were in the clear or not.

Two bulging canvas sacks with 'US Government' written across them in bold black letters were buckled in his saddlebags. Even without time for a count, Cort knew it would be a big payday for all four of them. As he rode ahead, the first rim of bright morning sun peeked over the craggy tops of Ceremonial Mountain, the old Indian encampment where the Crows came to worship Sun Gods, gathering every year at the beginning of spring. For now, Cort knew they were in the lead covering ground fast. That, at least, made him ride easier. He glanced back over his shoulder. Wic and Fan were still right there, staying close behind him. He slapped at the saddle-bags, flashing a quick smile. They were in the money and running free. It felt good.

Nate Whitman made his name as an uncompromising, hard nosed lawman who never gave up on anyone he was following. In the vast, unmapped stretches of the northern Rock Mountains, there was no law and no God west of Kansas. That wild land was every man for himself dispensing his own kind of justice either good or bad. Whitman, badge on his chest, felt it was his calling as a US Deputy Marshall, to enforce the law regardless of circumstances of time, distance, or danger. If it took him two weeks or two months to run down someone, he was willing to stay on it until successful. Although his home was in New Hope, he could and did travel far and wide tracking down men who thought they'd left any semblance of law far behind, only to look up from a flickering campfire or in some cow town bar, to see Whitman standing there stone-faced, six-gun drawn, ordering them to lift their hog leg out and drop it.

Tall, lanky to the point of looking almost skinny, he wore a tan wide-brimmed, high top hat with a deep crease right down the middle. His narrow, weathered face sported a big handlebar mustache peppered brown and silver suggesting his age. Whitman wore his six-gun high on his hip and always carried a Winchester lever rifle for a backup.

At various times he deputized other men to help form a posse, but did most of his tracking either alone or with the help of a young Mountain Crow lad he'd saved when just a child from a cavalry massacre of his tribe. The cavalry caught Black Antelope, chief of the Crows, right at dawn in their summer camp of over fifty teepees, attacking and killing men, women and even children as they stormed the encampment. Whitman found the six-year-old running for his life. He scooped him up, taking him to be raised on his ranch outside of New Hope. Now the young Indian had grown into his early twenties. Whitman named him Little Hawk, because of the circumstances he'd found him in. Whatever his true Crow name was he never asked or learned. The young man had inherited his keen, natural ability to track down men, white or brown, from his Crow ancestors. He and Whitman made a deadly team because of it.

It was admittedly a strange mix to see crusty, older Nate Whitman, over six feet tall, always accompanied by his shorter dark-skinned partner wearing white man's clothes, long black braids running down his back, his wide brimmed cowboy hat with a white-tipped eagle feather stuck in the band. If it seemed odd or funny to see the pair walking down the street in New Hope, no one dared bring it up when Whitman could hear them. They knew better.

The sun was well up when the lawman led his posse of ten men up on to the cliff rim before pulling to a stop. Nate only had to nod at tracks in the dust before Little Hawk got down, walking in a slow circle as his keen eyes studied the story written in dirt, while the rest of the men, still mounted, watched. When finished he looked up at the marshal.

'Four white men stop here. One stays behind before following. They go before sun up.'

'How can that kid know all that from a few tracks?' one man scoffed. 'What did they do, write down the time they left and how many they were? That's just Indian mumbo jumbo.'

Whitman turned to the man and his tired band of riders with a scowl. 'If Little Hawk says four men, it's four men. Can any of you read these tracks better? If you can't, keep your mouth shut and try to learn something!'

'Listen, Nate,' another pleaded. 'We've been riding all night busting our backs and we're no closer to that bunch now than we were back in New Hope. I've got a business to open this morning for God's sake. I can't keep on riding like you and that kid. I know some of the others feel the same way. If you're going any farther, you'll have to do it without me. You're getting paid for this. We're not.'

'Thomas is right,' a second man spoke up, pushing his hat back on his sweaty brow. 'I've got a wife and three kids to think about. We tried to help you out. We could have gotten shot or even killed if things went wrong. Think about that, too, Nate.'

The marshal eyed the riders circling around him with obvious contempt. He took in a slow breath trying to stay calm, looking at each man before speaking. 'If this stolen money hadn't come from the cavalry but from you or one of your businesses, would you still quit and run for home like a bunch of schoolboys? Even worse, what if the Kellers had taken the bank and cleaned out every dime leaving everyone in town flat broke? Would you all still be so worn out you can't ride another mile?'

'Wait a minute, Nate. That's not fair. We stuck our necks way out all night long because you asked for help. At least give us some credit for that. We're not gunfighters or a lawman like you. You ought to remember that.'

'I'll tell you what,' Whitman straightened up in the saddle. 'All of you turn your horses around and head back home. You're no good to me thinking you're doing me or yourself a favor. This bunch I'm after is likely to be the Kellers, from the description I got from the coach driver. If it is, they'll run long and hard. I can see none of you have the grit for it. I'll be better off without you.'

'You mean just the two of you are going to keep after them?' Thomas questioned.

'That's exactly what I mean. I'm wasting time now talking about it. When you get back to town tell my deputy Fulton, he's in charge until I return.'

'When do you think that will be?'

'I don't know yet. Little Hawk and I are going on a fast ride to see if we can catch up to them. It could be another two or three days. Now head for home like I said.'

Whitman and Little Hawk sat in their saddles watching the men pull their horses around starting away. The kid was first to comment in his half English lingo. 'White men care too much for their skin. My people never live by clock.'

'I'm a white man. You see me doing that?' Nate responded. 'They're just merchants and family men. I shouldn't have expected to get much more out of them than I did.'

'You different. You like Indian. You live outside on horse, ride far.'

'Yes, I guess you're right, Little Hawk. I've been that way since I was a boy. Let's get moving on these tracks and see if I'm right about the Kellers making them.'

*

Coy Brandon was at his Bluestone ranch standing next to the corral watching his son Colin trying to break a new rank horse he'd purchased in Janesville. The frantic animal bucked and leaped squealing loudly trying to throw the kid off its back, but he stuck like glue through sudden turns and twists before the horse launched itself back into the air.

'Stay on him, Colin!' Coy shouted encouragement, proud to see his son able to handle the frantic animal so skillfully. At fourteen Colin was already big for his age, nearly as tall at his father. His love for horses was only natural, growing up on the Wyoming Territory mountain ranch with Coy's penchant for buying and selling horse stock along with a few head of cattle he raised.

Neither the Brandon nor Keller families were born or raised in the territory. Their parents were originally from Tennessee, where they were farmers, raised hogs and horses, and where both were involved fighting for the Confederacy during the last brutal, bloody years of the Civil War. After the war ended, with the surrender of General Robert E. Lee at Appomattox Court House in 1865, an invasion nearly as bad as the war itself began. Northern carpetbaggers swept into a largely defenseless South, looting, ransacking and robbing personal items from farms and families. Horses, cattle, even the farm land and homes were often taken. Some owners were savagely beaten for information on whether or not family members were still fighting by joining small bands of renegade riders harassing Union supply lines and even killing Northern soldiers.

As young teenagers who had seen their families and homes destroyed, Cort, Red and Coy rode with some of those Southern raiders. When nothing was left but to flee the South, both families moved west, first into Kansas. After

12

several years they picked up again moving farther north into Wyoming Territory to get away from relentless persecution. The territory was wild, wide open, lightly peopled. The war had little presence or affect there except in newspapers.

Bitter memories of the war and the Southern invasion that followed were never forgotten by the three young men now in their mid-twenties. The robbery of the US pay wagon by Cort was just another act of revenge against a federal government he'd grown up to hate. Cort and Red had yet to marry, though both owned small plots of land and the sketchy beginnings of ranches near each other they hoped to build. Coy had on certain occasions ridden with his cousins on several earlier robberies. Now married and building a ranch while raising three young children, he'd stopped that wild and dangerous life at the pleading from his wife, Angelina. However he was still always willing to help his blood kin, offering fresh horses and even a hideout for a few days when they were on the run. He knew it could put him in jeopardy if caught, but his strong ties ran too deep to ignore.

By now Colin had the wild little mare finally worn down to running around the corral with only an occasional jump thrown in. 'She's ours now, Dad,' he smiled, riding by. 'One more time and she'll be ready to sell.'

'You did good!' Coy called out after him, turning from the pole-lined enclosure to see three riders emerging from dark timber across the meadow. He immediately recognized Cort in the lead. His big chestnut brown horse with a white blaze on its chest was a dead giveaway. Wic and Fan rode close behind him. Coy glanced at his large log house to see if Angelina was either outside or at the window. She wasn't. He thought it best. She wouldn't have time to get upset by Cort suddenly showing up.

13

'Feel like a little company?' Cort shouted, pulling to a stop and getting down.

'Any time, you know that.' They both shook hands before slapping each other on the back. 'You and those horses of yours look a little worn down. You aren't running from someone are you?' Coy half-kidded, pretty certain he already knew the answer.

'Yeah, we had to do a little night riding. You remember how much fun that is, don't you?'

'I sure do, if you want to break your neck and a horse's leg too. Who do you think might be coming behind you?'

Cort's half smile faded. 'Red will be here first, maybe in an hour or so. I left him to watch the back door, then catch up to us. Behind him I'm not sure yet. It might be Nate Whitman, and some hick town posse.'

Coy turned serious. So did his words. 'Whitman isn't some hick town sheriff, you know that. If it is him he won't turn back come hell or high water, as long as he has a track to follow. He takes that badge of his real serious. So should you. If he's the one, that's bad company.'

'I know that. That's why I left Red back there to be sure. When he catches up I'll know what we have to do.'

'If it is Whitman and that Indian kid of his, I might have to ask you to clear out a lot sooner than I'd like to. At least you know you can change to fresh horses.'

'Dad always told us to stick together. You know the old saying, blood's thicker than water?'

'Yes I do. Now I have a family of my own to think about and that's blood too. It's not like the old days when we were riding and running wild with no one to worry about but ourselves. Some day you'll know what I mean.'

'Maybe, but right now I'm not ready to rock the cradle just yet. What do you say we get to those fresh horses instead of standing here jawing about it.'

'Put your horses in the barn out of sight. I'll help you. While we're waiting for Red, they can get a good feed. So can you three in the house. Angelina will be surprised to see you again.'

The marshal and his young Crow sidekick followed tracks through hill country with increasing ease. As they rode, Whitman's mind worked trying to puzzle out where he thought the gang might be going. That's when he remembered an offhand conversation he'd had some months back with a friend who said that Keller had a cousin living somewhere near Janesville, in the general direction the tracks led. That simple disclosure suddenly became the key to unlocking Cort Keller's escape plans. Whitman pulled to a stop motioning for Little Hawk to do the same.

'If these tracks lead where I think they might, we may be facing even more guns than just Cort Keller and his gang. He could be heading for family. There's no telling how much more help he could get there. When we get close enough to know for sure, we'll lay up until dark before trying to smoke them out. That way they won't know how many guns they're facing.'

Little Hawk stared back before commenting. 'We not know either.'

'That's true, but I still believe that gives us the edge. Keep your eyes open up ahead for any sign of smoke or buildings. That's where we'll find this bunch. We don't want them to think we're within twenty miles until we make our move. This is one time Keller isn't going to ride away scot free like he has in the past. We'll bring him back to New Hope in cuffs or feet first. I don't much care which way either.'

CHAPTER TWO

Long shadows of evening crept over Coy Brandon's ranch, its silent fingers reaching out across the meadow into a dark band of timber on the other side. Inside the edge of those tall pines Whitman and Little Hawk silently watched the glow of kerosene lamps flicker on behind curtained windows inside the log-walled ranch house. No horses were tied out front at the hitching rail. A first curl of blue smoke twisted up from the stone chimney, as Angelina began cooking supper.

'They'll be eating soon,' the marshal whispered. 'We'll give them another ten minutes to get at the table, before moving in. You keep that six-shooter of yours real handy. If I know this bunch like I think I do, there'll be gunplay for sure. They're not going to just throw up their hands and quit.'

Little Hawk's hand moved down caressing the pistol grip on his wheel gun. His always stoic face lit with just the briefest flash of a smile. He loved the feeling of the big weapon. It excited him like nothing else could. The ancient Crow blood pulsing through his veins made his heart beat faster. His dark eyes never left the log house across the meadow. He was eager for a shootout. Whitman's hand grabbed his shoulder silently urging him to his feet. Both men stood for several minutes before starting across the meadow in slow motion, guns tight in their hands.

Inside the house Angelina brought a tray of smoking hot venison and potatoes to the table. Her dark brown eyes briefly met her husband's. That look said she was not happy to be feeding or hiding Cort and his men, but she would not say so out loud. To do so would bring on Coy's quick temper. She knew about the long, bloody history of fighting and robbery he'd once shared with his cousin before they met. It scared her when he first told her about his and his family's bitter days back in Tennessee, raiding and fighting against Union soldiers. It scared her even more now to have these dangerous men sitting in her house, at her table, with her children next to them.

'This dinner looks mighty fine, Angelina,' Cort's compliment broke the uneasy silence around the table.

'It sure does,' Red added, glancing at Wic and Fan. 'Sort of reminds me when we were back home in Tennessee and Mom's cooking.'

'Tennessee . . .' Coy's voice trailed off thinking about those wonderful teenage days before the ravages of war spread a dark cloud of misery over the South. 'I wonder what it's like back there now? We left a lot of friends when we moved west. Are they still there stuggling, or did they pull up and leave too?'

'Why talk about it now in front of the children?' Angelina spoke up irritated and worried the men would spend the entire evening reminiscing about the violence and killing, while Colin, Sallie Ann and Donetta listened.

Coy saw the nervousness and frustration in her eyes. He knew he had to change the conversation fast. 'Colin, the pitcher is nearly empty. Would you go out to the well and fill it up. Your dinner will stay hot if you move fast.'

'Sure Dad. I'll take care of it.' He came to his feet grabbing the large vessel.

'Better take the lantern and rifle too just in case,' Coy cautioned. 'That grizzly bear has been prowling around here the last few days near the horse corral.'

'I'll go with him to help out.' Wic quickly got to his feet. 'He'll have his hands full. I'll take the rifle, Colin.'

'All right.' Coy nodded, glad Wic offered, hoping Angelina would appreciate the gesture although she said nothing, continuing to serve each plate.

'Sounds like you're going to have to kill that bear,' Cort said. 'Once they get the smell of horse flesh up their nose it won't stop there. You know how those grizzlies are.'

'You're right. With everything else going on around here I haven't had the chance to get away and track him down. I know I'm going to have to. If you stay around a few days maybe we can both go after him.'

Outside in the dark, Whitman and Little Hawk approached the ranch house until only yards away. Suddenly the front door swung open and two figures stepped outside, backlit by lamp light, one carrying a long gun.

Whitman reacted quickly with a shouted order. 'Drop that rifle and put your hands up, or I'll cut you two down where you stand!'

Wic reacted instantly, shoving Colin out of the way. 'Get down, kid!' He brought the rifle up firing blindly at the voice the same instant the marshal and Little Hawk fired back. The .44 bucked in the young Crow's hands, shattering the lantern spewing a bright ball of flame over the ground illuminating the star man and his partner. Wic swung on Whitman diving for the ground, firing as fast as he could work the lever action. Little Hawk doubled-handed his pistol firing back at Wic, spinning him to the ground wounded. Colin lay a few feet away, belly crawling back for the door yelling for his father.

Cort, Red and Fan bolted from the table running to the door, pistols drawn, shouting for Wic. Coy grabbed his shotgun off pegs on the wall, slamming a window open and firing both barrels in the direction of two figures crouching in meadow grass. Angelina screamed, wrapping both arms around Donetta and Sallie Ann, pulling them down to the floor, covering their bodies with hers, petrified by the deafening gunfire.

'Get back. There's too many guns!' Nate grabbed the Crow by the shoulder pulling him to his feet, both men running into the night back toward dark timber, while bullets whined around them.

'Wic, are you hit?' Cort ducked outside as the shooting came to a sudden end, Red, Fan and Coy right on his heels.

Colin struggled to his feet. Coy ran up holding him at arm's length. 'Are you all right, son? Tell me you are!'

'My hands and face got a little burned when the lantern was shot out. Who fired on us? We haven't done anything wrong to anyone, have we Dad?'

'Don't worry about that right now. Get in the house and have your mother put something on those burns. She needs your help and needs to see you're not wounded.'

Cort kneeled next to Wic doubled up on the ground, trying to lift him into a sitting position. His hand felt the warm sticky blood of a bullet wound soaking through his shirt.

'Where are you hit?'

'In . . . my side. Feels like I'm . . . torn apart.'

'Red, Fan, help me get him inside where we've got some light,' Cort ordered.

At the table Cort swept dishes, knives and forks off with one sweep of his arm. Angelina stood against the wall with her arms around the children aghast at the scene, still trembling in fear from the sudden vicious attack.

Lifting Wic on the table, Cort carefully unbuttoned his shirt, opening it to see the ugly, bleeding bullet hole in his side just above his gun belt. He glanced up at his brother and Fan as Coy came to the table after escorting Angelina and the children into the bedroom.

'Wic needs a doctor, and fast or he'll bleed to death,' Cort said. 'There must be one in Janesville, isn't there?' He turned to Coy.

'There is, but he isn't going come all the way out here at this hour.'

'Then we'll take Wic to him. We can't do much out here on our own. You have a buckboard, don't you?' Coy nodded. 'Get the horses hooked up fast. You'll have to come with us to show me where he lives.'

'Don't go, Coy.' Angelina had exited the bedroom standing in shadows beyond lamp light. 'Give them the buckboard if we have to, but don't go. The law will think you're part of them. I can't live with that. I won't even try. Do you understand me?"

'Angelina, he's my cousin. I can't just walk away like that. You know better. You're just upset. It will pass. I'll be back soon as I can, you'll see.'

'I'm your wife, remember? And you have a family. You make a choice right now. Who is most important to you? Me and the children, or Cort. I'm not going to live like this and try to raise a decent family if you're going to be any part of this. I won't have the law coming out here threatening us for information or maybe even putting you in jail. I won't do it. I'll take the children and leave. I swear to God, I will. Our own son could have been killed out there tonight!' She buried her face in both hands crying.

'Wait a minute,' Cort put up both hands. 'I'll take care

of all this right now. We'll take the buckboard into town. You stay here with your wife, Coy. You can ride in tomorrow with Colin and bring it back out. Just help Red and Fan with the harness so we can get going. Does that suit you, Angelina?'

She stared back without comment, slowly nodding before turning for the bedroom, closing the door behind her. Coy turned to Cort, shrugging slightly embarrassed but thankful the confrontation had been avoided.

'I'm sorry. I guess she's right. I have to make a choice. Old habits die hard, you know that. We always did things together, sharing the good and bad, whatever came. I guess I can't have it both ways, anymore.'

'Don't worry about it, cousin. We'll always be blood. We'll get out of here fast. It'll make everything better for you.'

'Where are you headed?'

'I don't know yet. With Whitman on me I'll have to do some riding to shake him off. First I've got to get Wic to that doctor. It's likely I won't see you again for quite a while. Take care of yourself and your family too. Tell Angelina I'm sorry for the trouble I've caused. I never meant for any of it to happen here. You have to know that.'

'I do.' The two men shook hands before Cort pulled him closer, pounding his back and turning away without another word. Both men knew one of them might end up dead before that ever happened again but neither one said so out loud.

Whitman and Little Hawk ran across the meadow through darkened pines until reaching their horses. 'Where we go now?' his sidekick questioned.

'We're riding for Janesville so I can get some shooters who won't turn back the minute things get tough. New

21

Hope is too far away and takes too much time for that. I want to get up a posse before Keller can run again. He'll go even further now that he knows I'm trailing him. One thing I know for sure. We won't catch him flat like we just did at his cousin's ranch. Next time it will be a gun battle to the end, and I mean to end it once and for all.'

'This man can't ride anyplace with a wound like that,' Doctor William Whylie said in a steady professional tone, carefully wiping blood away from Wic's wound as he lay on his side on the examination table. 'I'll need to clean this out, see how deep the wound is, and stitch him up, if I can. It will take several days to see if the swelling and bleeding can be stopped.'

'We don't have any time for that,' Keller shook his head under the glow of lamp light hanging over the table. 'You'll have to do the best you can right here and now.'

'There's nothing fast about a bullet wound like this unless you want your friend to die in the saddle, if he isn't properly treated. You've gotten me up in the middle of the night at gunpoint demanding my help. I haven't even asked you how he was wounded, but I'd guess it wasn't cleaning his pistol. Now you don't want to take my advice on how to save him. If you insist on taking him with you he'll die a slow miserable death. That's the one thing I can promise you. Are you going to let me treat him or not? The choice is up to you and you don't need that six-gun to make it.'

Cort glanced at Red and Fan, their faces dark shadows under wide hats from the kerosene lamp burning brightly above. Neither spoke. Cort leaned down studying Wic's face, twisted in pain. 'What about it, Wic? We've got to clear out of here fast and ride. Are you up to it? If not just say so.'

Wic stared up with desperation in his eyes, pain written on his face, struggling to decide what to do. His hand gripped Keller's as he tried lifting himself slightly but fell back because of excruciating pain, his breath coming in short gasps.

'Don't . . . leave me here . . . alone. I'll try . . . to ride.'

'You heard him, Doc. Do the best you can and make it fast. You've got twenty minutes. Then we're leaving.'

'You just signed your friend's death warrant. I hope you understand that. I can't do much for him in twenty minutes. I might have to put him out just to clean this wound before I even start stitching him up.'

'You're wasting valuable time, Doc, get to it. You're the one on the clock.'

Keller's natural born slippery luck was still holding good.

At that same moment on the far end of town Nate Whitman was going from bar to gambling house trying to convince enough men to join him forming a posse. His luck was running the wrong way. Nighttime gamblers and drinkers didn't have any stomach or interest in leaving their preferred pastimes to go riding off into the night after someone most of them had never heard of, much less to get shot at. Whitman's frustration boiled over when he reached the Mountain House saloon. He climbed up on a small entertainment stage to berate the men who turned to watch him with his loud demanding voice.

'What's the matter with you men? Don't you care a whit about maintaining law and order? Do you want men like Keller and his gang running wild all over the country robbing and murdering innocent people? Where's your backbone!'

'Yeah, we might,' one man shouted back. 'We spend our time with friends, have a few drinks and don't bother anyone. We don't know this Keller you're so hot about. Long as he don't bother us, we got no reason to bother him!'

23

A roar of laughter and approval rose up from the crowd as the marshal stood, hands on his hips, staring back in disbelief.

The lawman wasn't done trying yet. 'If he and his gang come riding in here and start shooting up the town, you whiskey breaths will wish you helped out when you had the chance. This town has to have a sheriff. Where is he at? I'll get some real help while all of you sots stand around propping up the bar!'

Sheriff Mathew Buel heard incessant pounding on his front door, trying to ignore it until his wife, Lynette, demanded he get up answering it. Buel, fifty-one years old, was already considering retiring from the job. Staggering to his feet still in long underwear he headed for the door. Opening it, rubbing the sleep out of his eyes he found a pair of shady figures standing there. 'Mr, you better tell me Janesville is burning down to come here at this hour getting me up,' he threatened, irritated.

'I'm US Deputy Marshal Nate Whitman, from New Hope. I've got something just as important to tell you. Let me in.'

'Like what?' Buel still blocked the door unconvinced.

'Cort Keller and his gang are less than an hour's ride away from here. Me and my deputy, Little Hawk, just had a gun battle with the whole bunch at what I think is his cousin's ranch. I need you to get up a posse fast while Keller's still close. We might have wounded one of them. If we did, they could still be out there.'

'Well, Marshal Whitman, I don't care if you're chasing Flying Fox. I can't get a posse up in the middle of the night. Don't you know that? Maybe in the morning that might be possible, but not now. Everyone's still asleep except you two night owls.'

'By sunup Keller and his men can be twenty miles away

from here. I need men right now!'

'There aren't any men, I said. How many times do I have to explain that to you?' Buel's voice rose as his patience faded.

Whitman stood dumbfounded and exasperated. He was used to having his demands met quickly. He expected the same from another lawman. Instead all he got was excuses. His already frayed temper finally ran out.

'Do you have a deputy working for you?'

'I do.'

'I'll take him and you. Along with me and Little Hawk, that makes four of us. That's the best I can do right now. Go get him up and tell him to be ready to ride fast. I'm a US Marshal. My authority means I can demand help from local sheriffs. That means you. I'm ordering you to help me. If you refuse, I'll have you hauled into court for insubordination. Get dressed and let's get to it. I'm wasting time standing here arguing with you. Time is one thing I cannot waste!'

Buel stood for a moment trying to make sense of it all. Whitman and Little Hawk pushed right past him, inviting themselves inside before he could even answer. He started to say something then let it go. Turning back for his bedroom he mumbled something about madmen demanding the impossible in the middle of the night.

Cort, Red and Fan stood in shadows of Dr Wylie's living-room waiting for him to finish what he could do for Wic. Cort went to the curtained window parting it slightly, staring outside on to the darkened street.

Red pulled his pocket watch lifting it close enough to read the dial. 'It's been thirty minutes already. How much longer are you going to wait, Cort?'

'I'll give him a little more time. I need Wic with us if he

25

can ride.'

'I don't much like being cooped up here in town. We ought to be making tracks to someplace a long ways away from here,' Fan added his uneasiness.

'Neither do I, but I don't want to leave Wic flat. I know he'd do the same for either of us if. . . .'

The sound of fast-approaching hoofbeats stopped Cort's comments. He spread the curtains wider, seeing four riders flash by at a gallop. The unmistakable figure of Whitman's white dappled horse, Charger, led the way. Cort quickly stepped back, his voice tense with caution.

'That looked like Whitman right out there!' he whispered.

'Whitman? What's he doing here in town?' Red questioned.

'He sure didn't trail us here. Maybe he came in for more help. Now that we know where he is we'll ride in the opposite direction.'

'Like where?' Fan questioned, his hand fondling his six-gun.

'Maybe back toward New Hope. That's the last place he'd be looking for us.'

'Why go there?' Red's questioning tone made it clear he didn't like the idea one bit.

'Because we can do a little more "business", while the law is off chasing his tail, that's why. It depends on what Wylie can do for Wic, too.'

The three men stood in the dark without talking further, each to his own thoughts as minutes ticked away until Dr Wylie opened the door of the examination room stepping into the parlor. 'I've done all I can for your friend under these circumstances. The bullet went in below layers of skin creating a lot of damage and bleeding. If it had gone any deeper into the abdomen he'd be dead by now. That doesn't mean he's all right, just lucky on that count. He should have absolute rest and not pull those stitches out. If he does and starts bleeding again, he'll be in jeopardy of bleeding to death. I strongly suggest you put him up someplace where he can rest for at least two weeks to heal. He certainly shouldn't be in the saddle. Do I make myself perfectly clear?'

'Yeah, you do. What do I owe you, doc?' Cort's dismissive tone was short and to the point.

'After holding me at gunpoint, you now want to pay me?'

'That's what I said. How much?'

'If you're going to ride out of here and do what I think you are, you owe me nothing. All my work has been a waste of time and your friend's life. If you mean to give him a chance to recover, my fee for a bullet wound and stitching him up is thirty-five dollars.'

Cort reached into his jacket pulling out a wad of crisp new twenty dollar bills, courtesy of the US Cavalry payroll. Peeling off three he stuffed them into Wylie's pocket.

'I said thirty five, not sixty,' the doctor answered.

'The extra twenty is for the pistol I had to put on you. In case anyone asks, you can tell them I left a tip.' Cort turned to Red and Fan. 'Go in there and get Wic. Then let's get out of here.'

Once outside the men helped boost Wic up into the saddle. Cort stepped closer with one last word of warning. 'Doc says you can't bust those stitches loose or it's big trouble. We're heading back toward New Hope. Try to ride easy as you can and keep up. If you can't, let me know.'

Casner looked down, breathing heavily, fighting the searing pain. 'I'll try . . . let's get to it.' His voice was barely above a whisper.

Nate Whitman recklessly pushed his riders hard into the

night heading back to Coy's ranch. He was convinced if Keller wasn't still there, at least he might not have had enough time to get very far away, especially if he was carrying a wounded man as he thought he'd seen from the wild gunfight. The farther the four rode, the farther behind Buel and his young deputy, Jeff Banks, fell behind.

'Let that knothead kill himself,' Buel snorted to Banks riding next to him. 'Then we can go back to town and wait until dawn to get enough men to do a real tracking job, instead of this stupid idea.'

'I'd sure feel better if we had more men too,' Banks admitted, leaning low in the saddle, hanging on.

'General Whitman up there doesn't have any time for common sense. He thinks he's going to run this Keller bunch down in the dark. I tried to explain it to him, but he's too thick-headed to listen. When we get to Brandon's ranch, I'll try to talk to Coy before Whitman goes off shooting up the place. I know him a little bit and he's never given me any trouble before. I don't think he will now either. That is, if I get the chance.'

CHAPTER THREE

Angelina and the three children were already in bed asleep, but not her troubled husband. He sat at the kitchen table under a single coal oil lamp still thinking about the sudden savage gunfight that had his family scared, upset and in fear there would could be more to come. He loved Angelina more than life itself. She'd changed him in ways he never thought possible. But his strong blood connection to Cort went all the way back to Tennessee, and both their families too. Back to a time when he lived the wild life just as Cort did, raiding, robbing, harassing Union troops and fighting the carpetbaggers that followed, who took everything they held dear until they were forced to flee their very homes and the South they'd always known and loved.

Now Cort was in big trouble with the law again. Coy's emotions were torn right down the middle because of it. He closed his eyes, resting his head in both hands, his mind swirling with indecision.

His thoughts were suddenly interrupted by the sound of fast hoofbeats coming closer. Was Cort returning for some reason, or was it more trouble with the law? He couldn't be sure after a night like this.

He got to his feet grabbing the shotgun off wall pegs next to the door. Lifting the lamp from its hook over the table, he went to the door opening it just a crack trying to see outside as four shadowy figures pulled their horses to a stop.

Whitman was first off his horse, already shouting orders. 'You in the house, come out unarmed with your hands in the air. If you refuse I'll burn you out!'

Buel, who had already had enough of Whitman's orders for the night ran up behind the marshal, grabbing him by the shoulder spinning him around. 'For God's sake, get hold of yourself. There are likely women and children in there. I know this man. Let me try to talk to him before you do something you'll regret.'

'And there could also be Keller or some of his men in there too. Take your hands off me or I'll cuff you first!'

'Have you gone mad? You're letting your anger overrule common sense. You're not carrying out any kind of law. You're doing this for pure revenge. I'll stop you any way I can. I won't be a part of this. It's murder while hiding behind a bloody badge!'

The two star men began struggling, but Little Hawk quickly moved up behind Buel. Lifting his pistol high over his head the Crow deputy brought it down crashing on the sheriff's skull, knocking him unconscious to the ground.

Young Banks ran forward trying to help, but Little Hawk quickly turned, leveling his wheel gun menacingly. 'Give me gun, or I take it,' he ordered, advancing on Banks until the young lawman felt the cold steel of a pistol shoved hard into his stomach. 'Do not interfere with us, young man,' Whitman warned. 'or you'll get the same as your boss did. Give him your gun, now!'

Little Hawk pulled the six-gun from Banks' holster, shoving him back a few steps. 'You no move,' he ordered in his pidgin English, his intent clear enough to stop him.

Nate Whitman advanced on the ranch house demanding again that Coy step out with both hands up and empty. Coy could only vaguely see the struggle and hear the sound of what had taken place in the brief confrontation between the four men. Confused by it, he yelled out from behind the door.

'Who is out there? What's going on? Speak up or you'll get a load of shotgun!'

'This is US Marshal Nathaniel Whitman. I'm ordering you to give up and get yourself out here now. I won't ask again!'

'Whitman? You've caused enough misery for one night. Cort isn't here. Neither are any of his men. Saddle up and ride out of here. Leave us alone. My family and I aren't bothering anyone. I've done nothing wrong.'

The marshal turned to his partner with an order. 'Get me something I can burn. Brush, a limb, anything.'

'You can't do that,' Banks protested, holding up both hands.

'You shut up and stay out of the way. Little Hawk, cuff him after you get me that firewood. I don't want any more interference from either of these two.'

Coy still stood behind the door for protection, tightly gripping his shotgun, until he saw the flare of a match followed by brighter flames of the ignited torch. Whitman advanced closer shouting his threat to burn it down. Coy had to do something and fast. His wife and children were all he could think about. Kicking the door open he stepped outside, shotgun still in one hand, raising the other to stop and talk. Before he could speak, Whitman dropped the torch, leveling his six-gun on him firing once, twice and a third time, crumpling Coy to the ground. Whitman ran forward, Little Hawk right behind him until both stood over Brandon.

'Roll him over and get that shotgun before I cuff him,' the marshal ordered.

The Crow deputy pulled Coy over by his shoulder. In flickering firelight of the still burning torch, he leaned lower.

31

'No need cuffs. You shoot him dead, already.'

Whitman turned walking up to Jeff Banks. His voice was a low, menacing order. 'If anyone asks you, Brandon aimed his shotgun on me and I had to stop him or be killed myself. Understand me?'

'But he didn't do that. You shot him down in cold blood. I saw how it happened.'

The marshal grabbed Banks by the jacket yanking him up face to face. 'I said he had that shotgun on me first. You try to say any different, you'll end up the same way. I'm not going to have some two-bit Southern rebel ignore the law and not pay for it. Do as you're told, or I'll personally see to it you end up without a badge or job!'

Buel staggered to his feet holding his bloody head, trying to make some sense out of the confusion around him. Coy lay a few feet away. His deputy came to his side, helping him steady himself. 'What . . . happened . . . who hit me?'

'You got out of line,' the marshal answered. 'I had to have Little Hawk stop you before you did something you'd regret. I'm running the show here and no one else. Don't you or Banks forget it. Brandon tried to kill me. I had to stop him. Didn't I, deputy?' He eyed the young deputy who only stared back without answering.

A sudden cry of anguish turned all four men to the front door. Angelina, still in her nightgown, stood trembling, both hands to her mouth, terrified at the sight of her husband lying a few feet away. She ran forward, collapsing on top of him sobbing uncontrollably.

'Coy, Coy, don't die on me!' She looked up at Whitman, pleading through a tear-streaked face, cradling Coy's head in her arms. 'You murderer, you killed my husband. I saw what you did!'

Buel finally regained his senses enough to walk up to the marshal, still holding the back of his head with one hand.

'Is this what you call justice? You just turned that badge you're wearing into a blood red star. Everyone will know it soon enough if I have my way.'

'You better get used to it. This is how you stop these Johnny rebs.'

After a week of hard riding north up in the lofty Big Sheep Mountains, Captain Theodore Criswell, of the 77th Cavalry, sat in his freshly pitched tent reading a message just brought to him by a courier out of Fort Jackson. The young private delivering it stood at attention while Criswell digested the note. Ending it with an audible sigh, he looked up at the man in blue.

'Did they tell you back at Fort Jackson, this message was so urgent they had to send you all the way up here to deliver it?'

'No sir. They just ordered me to get it to you fast as possible. It took me two extra days riding to find you up here.'

'I see. Get yourself and your horse a good feed. I'll send you back tomorrow with my reply.'

'Yes sir.' The private saluted smartly turning to exit the tent as Criswell went over the note a second time, pulling at his chin.

> From Command, Fort Jackson
> May 27, 1867
> To Captain Theodore Criswell

> This message is to inform you that the United States Cavalry courier pay wagon was stopped and robbed at gunpoint by four men on May 5, thought to be the Keller gang, near New Hope. You are ordered to relieve your unit of six men to ride to New Hope, to see what they can further learn and also the possible

whereabouts of these men. Any further information learned there should be brought to us by a pair of your fastest riders. You are to remain with your main unit continuing to pursue the Northern Cheyenne Indians who have been raiding in the Big Sheep Mountains.

I remain,

Commander Judson P. Weatherly

Fort Jackson, Wyoming

Criswell got to his feet, walking to the open tent flap looking out on his new encampment. The large, green meadow only yards away was split by a small crystal clear creek gurgling over rocks. Beyond, a picket line of horses fed steadily on lush green grass in front of white canvas tents while some troopers uniformed in blue tended smoking campfires. Others took the brief rest to sit cleaning their Springfield 45-55 carbines after the long ride into the mountains. It all seemed so idyllic, peaceful, yet trying to trail up the elusive, dangerous Cheyenne could change in seconds to an all-out ambush. Criswell didn't like the idea of splitting up his command. He might need every single man and rifle available if things suddenly turned into a savage gun battle. Yet orders were orders, and he had no choice but to obey them. His orderly was busy a few yards away stacking fresh firewood for the evening campfire. The captain called him over.

'Yes sir?'

'I want you to fetch Sergeant O'Halloran. Tell him to come over here on the double.'

'Right away, sir.'

Criswell went back inside his tent, sitting down until the sergeant came up. He waved him in. It only took a brief glance to see why O'Halloran had been promoted to sergeant. Grady O'Halloran looked like a man who meant to have his own way come hell or high water. Standing just five foot nine, the ruddy faced Irishman's broad brawny shoulders filled out his blue tunic, nearly bursting stitches. His square-jawed face sprouted unshaven red whiskers around a straight slit mouth, used to barking orders that better be obeyed. If not they would be settled out behind camp with his hard knuckled fists. He was the perfect man to maintain order especially out on dangerous patrol like this where men had to follow orders to stay alive and not panic under ambush or attack.

'You called for me, Captain?'

'I did. I have a somewhat unusual job for you to do. There's been a robbery of our pay wagon back near New Hope. I want you to choose five men, your best riders, and leave for there today. Get as much information as you can about the robbery including talking to the marshal there. What's his name... Whitman? Command believes the Keller gang are the ones who robbed the courier. Whatever information you get, send two fast riders back to Fort Jackson with it, then get back here. Take one of our Crow scouts with you so you can find us when you return. We'll be moving farther back into these mountains. You'll need him for that.'

'All that's going to take some time, sir.' O'Halloran was already skeptical about his new orders. 'I might not get back here for a week, if that.'

'I know that, Sergeant. That's why you better get cracking. Pick your men and get extra rations from the supply wagon. I want you out of here in one hour.'

Cort's bold plan to quickly double back to New Hope, began to unravel because of Wic Casner's bleeding wound. That first day on the trail even riding at a slower pace didn't help. The fresh stitches pulled and tore at Wic's side until bleeding started again. He tried not to complain but by late that afternoon he'd had enough and was forced to pull to a stop. Cort, in the lead, wheeled his horse around, riding back.

'I think I'm going to have to stop.' Casner opened his jacket revealing his bloody shirt. 'Maybe it might be better if you three go on ahead. I'll try to catch up later after I rest a while. I don't want to mess up your plans, but I won't be much help like this.'

Cort glanced at his brother Red, then Fan. Neither said a word until Red spoke up. 'If Wic says he can't help us, I think we ought to at least try to find someplace where he can hole up. The three of us can go into town and take care of business on our own if we have to. Then maybe we can pick up Wic and get out of here.'

'Maybe, but where can he hole up?' Tyge questioned.

An uneasy silence fell over the three men until Wic spoke up. 'I used to work at the old Corker silver mine. I might still have friends there. It's far enough out of town no one would come poking around. This bleeding isn't going to stop until I get off this horse and stop riding. Why don't we give it a try there, Cort?'

'All right. We'll swing east to the mine when we get closer. Just the three of us in town, instead of four, changes everything, but there's nothing anyone can do about it.'

Evening stars were already beginning to dot the dusky sky when the riders came out of timber on to a rutted road leading up to the mine. Ahead they saw dim lights from several shacks where workers bunked. 'How you doing, Wic?' Cort twisted in the saddle as they rode up on the first rickety building.

'I'm about played out. I think you'll have to help me

down or I'll tear more stitches loose.'

A door creaked open. The figure of a bearded man stepped out, holding a lantern, trying to see the sudden intruders. 'Who are you? What do you want?'

Wic studied the silhouette a moment. 'Carl, Carl Loney, is that you?'

The old man stepped closer lifting the lantern. 'Well I'll be damned. Wic Casner, I haven't seen you in a coon's age. What are you doing back here?'

'He needs someplace to rest up a while and heal where no one will question him about it,' Keller interrupted. 'He's carrying a bullet wound.'

'Bullet wound? What have you been doing to end up with something like that, Wic? You got the law on you?'

'We don't have time to answer a lot of questions. All I want to know is if he can hole up here a while, and you keep it quiet,' Cort demanded.

'Well, yeah, I can. Get him off that horse and inside.'

Keller and Red helped Wic into the dingy shack while Tyge carried his saddle-bags.

'You lay low while we do a little business in town. If we don't come back right away don't worry about it. We might have to do some traveling then swing back depending on whether or not someone is on us, like Whitman. Get as much rest as you can and be ready to ride when we show up,' Cort said.

Reaching into his pocket he pulled out a leather wallet fat with cash. Peeling off four twenties, he handed them to Loney. 'You get him whatever he needs with this. There should be enough money to last until we get back here.'

The white-haired old man nodded, eyes wide on the cash. 'I'll do what I can. Wic's an old friend. I sorta took him under my wing when he was younger. I just hope you boys ain't into too much trouble, that's all.'

37

'No more than usual,' Red spoke up, a wry smile crossing his face. They shook hands all around before exiting the cabin.

'What now?' Tyge questioned outside.

'With Wic out I'm going to have to roll the dice. Three of us instead of four makes a difference. I'll ride into town alone early tomorrow to be certain Whitman hasn't made it back yet. If it looks clear I'll have you two come in one at a time. I don't want anyone getting suspicious about three riders together after the courier payroll we took. I might even rent us a room for a couple of days while I look over the bank. When I get done in New Hope, I'll make Nate Whitman look like some kid wet behind the ears with a badge he can't back up. Especially after what he did at Coy's ranch. I'll make him pay for that as long as he draws a breath or wears that tin star of his.'

Leroy Fulton, Nate Whitman's young deputy, walked down the morning streets of New Hope with a swagger of authority in his step. The marshal gone, at least for a while, and for the first time he was the town's only law. Whitman himself had ordered it to his returning posse. He relished not being ordered around and sometimes even belittled by his always critical boss. Being top dog at last, he'd never felt more important or needed. He meant to savor every single minute of it.

A few businesses were just opening with most still closed for another hour. The boardwalks were nearly empty too. The only other person on the street was a lone rider that Fulton studied a moment, then nodded at as he passed. Cort Keller did the same without looking back. Fulton did notice the rider's big, grey roan horse looked like a real runner with its sleek body and long legs. After that his thoughts went back to how authoritative and in charge he should carry himself. He secretly hoped Whitman and Little Hawk would stay gone a month.

'Good morning, Leroy,' a store owner smiled, unlocking the front door to his shop. 'Heard anything from Nate, yet?'

'No, him and that Crow kid of his are still gone, but I'm taking care of things until he gets back. You don't have to worry none about anything like that.'

'Oh, I'm sure you are. I was just wondering about him that's all. Time I open up. I'll see you later today when you make your rounds.'

'You can bet on it.' Fulton strutted away down the boardwalk noticing up ahead the man on the roan horse had pulled to a stop in front of a small eatery, getting down to go inside. He quickened his step. It was his job to keep an eye on everything, and that included strangers. He decided to jaw with the man a few minutes just to let him know who was in charge in town.

Cort was already at a table near the window, sipping a fresh cup of steaming hot coffee when Fulton pushed through the door.

'Morning, Leroy.' The owner looked up from totaling last nights tickets. 'You want the usual?'

'No, I'll just have a quick coffee. I've still got the rest of town to walk.'

Fulton took the cup in one hand, eyeing Cort and starting for his table. 'Mind if I sit down?' He came up to Keller.

Cort, who was trying to ignore the star man, looked up. 'No, I don't mind.'

Leroy eased into a chair studying the stranger, both men locking eyes with each other. 'You must be new in town. I've never seen you before.'

'Just passing through.' Cort wasn't going to say any more than he had to.

'On the drift, huh?'

'That's about it.'

'I'm the deputy here.' Leroy pointed to the badge pinned on his vest. 'It's my job to know what's going on and who is doing it. I don't mind drifters unless we've got paper on them. This is a peaceable town and we mean to keep it that way. How long do you mean to stick around?'

'Only a day or two.'

'I'll keep count on that, Mr. . . ?'

'Johnson, Bill Johnson.'

'All right, Mr. Johnson.' Fulton pushed to his feet, taking one more long look at the man with green eyes and sandy colored hair. 'I'm glad we understand each other. We do, don't we?'

'We sure do.'

'Good enough.' Fulton headed for the door, stepping outside. Cort watched him go before getting up and paying for his coffee.

'What time does the bank open?' He asked the cookie.

'Nine o'clock, during the week, but they're closed on Saturday and Sunday.'

'Thanks,' Cort started for the door.

'I serve up a real good lunch and dinner too,' the owner called after him. 'You might want to give them a try. It's the best in town.'

'I didn't see any other diner when I rode in.'

'You're right. There isn't any other. That why I can say it's the best in town.' He laughed at his own joke.

CHAPTER FOUR

Cort crossed the street entering the Timber Jack Hotel, taking a room for three nights on the second floor directly across the street from the Miner's Mercantile Bank. From his vantage point he could keep track of exactly the time the bank opened, if they employed a guard at the front door, and when the flow of people in and out was lowest.

After two days studying the layout, that afternoon he boldly crossed the street stepping inside the bank for a moment, looking everything over before riding out of town to bring in Red and Tyge. Once all three were back in his room, he laid out his plan to take the bank, in a low, insistent voice to be certain he was being clearly understood.

'The bank opens at nine o'clock sharp every morning. That's when most of the businessmen make their cash deposits. They have one guard. He opens up then stands at the door for early customers before moving inside next to it. Their slow time is late afternoon. That's when we'll move on them. Red, soon as we enter you cover the guard and disarm him. Tyge, you take care of the cage clerks. There's two of them. I'll get inside the cage and make the bank manager open the vault if it isn't already open. After sacking up the money, we'll lock all of them in the vault. That gives us plenty of time to get out of town before

41

anyone knows what's happened. You two got the picture? It's the timing that's important. We have to move fast and smart.'

'What about Wic?' Red questioned. 'Are we going to go get him?'

'I'll leave him where he is for now. He won't be ready to make a long run yet. He needs more rest. I'll fetch him later.'

'Where we heading after we take the bank?' Fan asked. 'We can't go back to Coy's, can we?'

'No, we can't. I've already gotten him in enough trouble I didn't mean to. I'm not about to do that to him twice. We'll ride south into mesa country. If Whitman even tries to follow us down there tracking over that hard, dry ground makes it almost impossible.'

Sergeant O'Halloran and his five cavalrymen galloped into New Hope early that same afternoon causing a stir from people on the street because of the recent robbery of the government pay wagon and subsequent activity from the 77th Cavalry that followed.

Red, sitting at the window in the hotel room, saw the line of soldiers and quickly called for Cort and Fan. 'Would you look at that. What's the US Cavalry doing riding in here in such a big hurry? Could them showing up change our plans, Cort?'

'We don't have time to change plans. But we'd better keep an eye on them so we don't end up in the same place at the same time. I still mean to take the bank. I didn't plan all this to walk away from another big pay day because of a couple of blue coats. Fan, go downstairs and see where they go, then get back up here. I want to know what they're doing.'

Sergeant O'Halloran pulled to a halt in front of the

marshal's office, ordering his men to wait outside in their saddles.

'Private Varney, find a livery stable and get these horses watered and fed. All of you men wait there until I show up.'

'Yes sir,' Varney gave a half-hearted salute, tired and dusty from the long fast ride to reach town from Big Sheep Creek.

O'Halloran mounted steps pushing the door open into the office to find Leroy Fulton sitting with his feet up on the desk. The moment Leroy saw the cavalry blue uniform, he pulled them down, sitting up. The sergeant skeptically studied the deputy a moment before speaking.

'You aren't Whitman, are you?' The tone of his voice made it clear he didn't believe his own question.

'No, I'm his deputy.' He came to his feet. 'Leroy Fulton's my name. Marshal Whitman is away trailing what he believes to be the Keller gang. I'm the law here in town until he gets back. What can I do for you?'

'I'm not sure you'll do, at all.'

'Do for what?'

'My orders are to learn as much as I can about the payroll robbery from this Whitman. With him not here, it looks like I've made a long ride for nothing.'

'I know a few things about the robbery,' Leroy protested. 'Ask me.'

'You do, huh? We'll see about that. Captain Crisswell wants to know for sure it was the Keller gang that pulled it off and where Whitman thinks they might be now. Neither me or my men have been paid because of those Johnny rebels. That makes it even more personal. If I could get my hands on Keller I'd put a rope around his neck and swing him right here on main street. Do you at least know when Whitman might get back here?'

'No, I don't. Only him and Little Hawk are still after

43

them. He's already sent back the posse he had. I do know if he's got a trail to follow he'll likely stay on it. Why don't you stay here in town a couple of days and see if he comes in? Then you can ask him.'

O'Halloran pulled at his stubbled chin mulling over the idea. He was still under orders to send two of his men back to Fort Jackson, with new information, but he had none to send. The pained expression on his face made it clear he wasn't sure what to do. A few days in town might solve that if the marshal did show up. He had another idea too.

'You got a bank here?'

'Sure. The Miner's Mercantile. It's two blocks down the street on this side. Why are you asking?'

'Because I just might go down there and see if maybe there's any government money in it. There might be something left over from last month. I can't have my men and myself waiting around here without two bits in our pockets. We've got to eat and have a place to stay even for just a few days. That takes cash.'

'I'm about to make my afternoon rounds. Come on, I'll walk you down to the bank.'

Up in the hotel room Cort went over plans one more time to be certain there were no questions. "You both understand this? We have to move fast and make no mistakes. We work together, it goes off smooth,' he looked from Red to Fan, both men nodding. 'Then let's get to it. We want to take the bank quietly without gunfire if we can. Any shooting only brings us trouble. Tyge, bring the horses around in front of the bank and tie them off. I'll give you ten minutes, then we'll all meet across the street and take care of business.'

Cort and Red busied themselves packing saddle-bags, leaving the window unattended at the same moment the sergeant and deputy walked down the street and pushed through the front door of the bank. Fan brought the horses around from the alley behind the hotel crossing the street in front of the bank and looping the reins over the hitching post. The brothers exited the hotel walking directly across the street to meet him. Cort looked briefly at both men. His voice was low, steady, calm. 'Let's do it.'

The three stepped inside the bank, pulling six-guns on seeing the guard, an older man, with his back to them talking to Deputy Fulton. At one of the teller's cages Sergeant O'Halloran stood questioning the clerk about any possible money, in his usual loud voice.

Cort hesitated a split second with the unexpected presence of both the deputy and cavalryman, armed, standing only feet away. Their well-rehearsed plans suddenly went out the window. Red realized it too, quickly swinging his pistol barrel down hard on the guard's head knocking him to the floor unconscious. Fulton froze, eyes grew wide with fear. His mouth fell open staring back at Cort's six-gun leveled on him belt high.

'You . . .' his voice trailed off.

'Yeah. The name is Cort Keller. Sound familiar? Pull your pistol and drop it on the floor. Two fingers. If I see any more than that I'll drop you where you stand!'

'Don't do it!' O'Halloran shouted, suddenly lunging at Fan, both men wrestling up against the counter until Tyge fired a single shot sending the blue coat crashing to the floor with a bullet ripping across his back.

Fulton stood paralyzed with fear. His hands trembled as his mind spun with indecision. This was the only chance he'd ever have to become a real hero. All he had to do was pull his six-gun and fire fast enough to save all of them even though he'd never pulled a gun on anyone before in his entire life. His hand moved hesitantly down to the gun belt

45

until Cort's voice stopped him.

'Two fingers. You pull it and you're a dead man. Do it now!'

Fulton stabbed at the pistol in wild desperation. The thunderous report of Cort's pistol sent the deputy spinning to the floor screaming in pain, grabbing his stomach.

Cort retrieved Fulton's pistol, shoving it into his own gun belt. 'Get that blue coat's weapon too,' he shouted to Fan. 'Red, lock the door. Don't let anyone in!'

Keller vaulted over the counter ordering the two clerks up against the wall, ordering Fan to cover them before dragging the bank manager out from under his desk where he'd hidden. Pulling the bald-headed man up face to face, he gave a quick order.

'Open the vault or you'll never live to spin the dial twice!'

Inside the money room Cort made the manager stuff three heavy canvas bags with gold and silver coins. 'No paper money,' he threatened. When finished he had the man double tie the bag tops. 'Get over in that corner and stay there. Red, Fan, get the rest of them in here including Fulton and the sergeant. Have the tellers drag them if you have to.'

Once the brick lined room was full, Keller started the heavy steel door swinging shut with a final order. 'You tell Whitman, Cort Keller was here while he was off chasing his tail. Tell him he'll never be smart enough to catch up to me no matter what he tries!'

The instant the vault door clanged shut, the three men ran for the front door. Unlocking it Cort opened it only far enough to peek out. Two men and a woman stood outside waiting patiently in line to enter. He glanced back at the pair. 'We'll walk out of here real easy like and get to the horses. Let me do any talking. Let's move.'

Stepping outside the first man in line immediately questioned Keller. 'Why is the bank door locked at this hour?'

'They're doing some bookwork on money losses. They won't be open for another hour. We couldn't even deposit our cash.' He held up one of the money bags.

'But that will be too late,' the lady spoke up.

'Sorry, ma'am. They said they've got a lot of figuring to do.'

The three men climbed in saddles, starting away leaving customers standing on the boardwalk wondering what was going on. The man at the head of the line gingerly reached for the door knob. Turning it open he stuck his head inside far enough to see red smears of blood across the floor, before he began yelling for help while Cort, Red and Fan kicked their horses into a gallop riding out of sight at the far end of town.

'They walked into the bank . . . and started shooting . . . at me and your deputy.' Sergeant O'Halloran lay on a cot face down, in back of the marshal's office as a doctor worked on his back while Nate Whitman stood at his side. 'We never had a chance to . . . stop them . . . one of them shot me in the back. They killed your deputy . . . too.'

The marshal straightened up, his face a grim mask of frustration and defeat. Keller had outsmarted him again, doubling back to his own town while he was out riding after shadows. He knew everyone in town would be talking about it too. He tried consoling himself that at least he'd gotten Coy Brandon. The whole sordid story wasn't a complete loss.

Later that same evening he sat in his office trying to plan his next move, when his luck took a sudden turn for the better. A scruffy looking man pushed through the door, checking behind him to be sure he wasn't seen or followed.

Garrett Wilson, who worked at the Corker silver mine, eyed the star man warily as he approached the desk with a strange tale to tell but for a price.

'I got something of value you might wanna know, but you gotta promise not to ever tell who you heard it from. I don't want no accidental dynamite charge to go off on top of me next I'm down in a hole working.'

Whitman leaned forward wondering what the sudden interruption was all about. 'If you've got something to say don't waste my time. Spit it out. What are you talking about?'

'I'm talking about four men who rode up to the mine a few days back during the night. One was wounded in some kind of gunfight. He's staying in the shack next to me, trying to heal up, with a man named Carl Loney who works out there too. No one's supposed to know about it but I heard them because I was still up. I heard one of them call out to someone named Keller. Ain't that the name of the gang that robbed the mail coach?'

Nate eyed the man with sudden interest. If what he was saying was the truth, it could change the entire outcome, finding and finishing off the Keller gang once and for all, restoring his reputation at the same time.

'Which shack does this Loney live in?' he asked.

'Last one on the right when you ride up to the mine. The main office sits behind it about fifty feet away. Mine is next to it on the left. If you decide to come out be sure you don't shoot my place up too. I don't want to get hit by no stray bullets – know what I mean?'

'You're certain this man is still there, is that what you're telling me?'

'Yup. He was there an hour ago when I rode in. When do you think you might want to make your move?'

'I'll keep that to myself. You just stay out of the way the

48

next couple of days.'

'Oh, you don't have to worry none about that. I ain't gettin' mixed up in any gunfight. I was thinking I might want to ask you for some kind of payment for me tellin' you all this. But now I decided not to. I just want to be a good citizen.'

'Sure, you do. Now get out of here and keep your mouth shut. I don't want any chance this gets back to the wrong people. You understand me?'

Near midnight the dark silhouette of two riders pulled to a stop on a bend in the mine road, short of the cabins. Marshal Whitman made a silent gesture with his hand to get down. He and Little Hawk tied off the horses and started up the road on foot. Whitman counted four workers' shacks. The window of the one on the far right was lit by the dim glow of lamp light. He pulled his Crow deputy up close. 'That's the one,' he whispered. 'When I go in you stay right behind me.'

Little Hawk said nothing, his dark eyes riveted on the low dwelling for any sound or image moving across the window. He lifted his pistol out, cocking the hammer back as Whitman closed the distance.

'You feeling any better?' Loney turned to Wic who was lying on a bunk over on one wall, shirt off, his stomach wrapped in makeshift bandages. On top of a small table next to him his gunbelt lay coiled up.

'It's slow going. If I don't move around too much it's better. But I know I sure couldn't ride anyplace yet. I'd just start bleeding all over again.'

'Then it's best you just keep resting up. Your friends won't likely be back for a while. I guess the longer that is, the better for you, huh?'

49

'I'd like to be in the saddle on the move. That's what all of us are good at. Staying in one place too long usually means trouble can catch up to you. Right now I've got no other choice.'

'Can I ask you why or how you turned to robbing and whatever else you had to do to live like that? I never thought of you as some kind of wild kid. What drove you to it?'

'You didn't live back in Tennessee, like our families did when the war ended. You don't know what Union soldiers did to us and the scum that followed them. Cort and Red saw it just like me and my family did. Fan was never a part of it. Cort took him on because he's good with a gun and not afraid to use it. But us three had a lot to get even with the government over. This is how we try to even that score just a little bit. We never wanted any part of them or their rules and laws. That's the main reason why.'

'I don't know, Wic. Seems like a good way to get yourself either shot or hung. Maybe I'm too old or a coward, but I just don't think there's any future in living that way.'

The marshal and Crow edged quietly up to the shack. Whitman slowly pressed his face to the window peering through the edge of the curtain into the small room. He saw Wic laying on the bunk, but not Loney, although he could hear him talking. He turned to Little Crow, holding up two fingers, before pulling him close.

'When we rush the door I'll take the one laying on the bed. You take whoever the other one is. I can't see if he's armed or not. Don't take any chances with either of them.'

The deputy nodded, gripping his pistol tighter. Whitman grabbed the door handle twisting and slamming it open in one quick motion, rushing into the room.

'Hands up!' He shouted, pistol aimed arm's length on Casner.

50

Wic lunged for his pistol on the table. Whitman fired once, twice, in quick succession. Wic's body jerked at bullet hits, still struggling to reach his gun before he went limp, sliding on to the floor. Loney, scared to death by the sudden, savage entrance, tried diving under the table for cover. Little Hawk's six-gun spit fire and lead, hitting the old man in the neck and head, killing him instantly too, tipping the table over and breaking the coal oil lamp on the floor with an explosion of spreading flame.

The marshal straddled Wic's body pulling him up to see if he was still alive. One quick look was all it took to see Cort Keller's trusted cousin was a dead man.

'What about the old man?' Nate shouted over fast-spreading flames.

'He dead too.'

'Then let's get out of here and let the whole place burn down.'

'What about the men?'

'Let both of them burn in hell along with it!'

CHAPTER FIVE

A pair of cavalry troopers rode dangerously close along the narrow canyon trail above a roaring, white water river far below. Ahead, a quarter mile away, they saw Captain Criswell's line of men climbing toward a gun sight pass to top out.

'There they are!' One rider pointed ahead. 'I'm sure glad we found the captain without another five days riding in Crow territory. I don't want to stay in here any longer than we have to. I was about ready to turn back and say we couldn't find him.'

'Sir, riders coming in,' Lieutenant Martin Stanford, riding next to Captain Criswell, pointed to riders climbing towards them. Criswell held up his hand, stopping his line of troopers.

'What in God's name are those two doing following us all the way in here?' He turned to Stanford. The look on Criswell's face made it clear he wasn't happy about it. 'I don't like surprises, and I think I'm about to get one I didn't ask for.'

The cavalrymen pulled to a halt saluting, handing the captain a hand written note. 'We were sent to find you by Sergeant O'Halloran, sir.'

'O'Halloran?' Criswell cut him off before he could

explain further. 'Why didn't he come himself?'

'Sir, the sergeant is still in New Hope. He's been badly wounded. He tried to stop a bank robbery in town and got shot in the back. He sent us after you to tell what happened. He wants you to know the Keller gang took the bank. They killed the deputy sheriff there, too. He thinks command might change your orders to turn around and go after Keller.'

If the captain was irritated about being stopped, his patience ended with this final suggestion. 'Sergeant O'Halloran does not give orders to anyone but the men under him. Certainly, he cannot suggest what I do as his commanding officer. I'm concerned to hear he was wounded, but until or unless I get direct orders from Fort Jackson, I cannot simply turn my men around and start chasing after this Keller bunch. You men are now back in my command. Take your place in line.'

Criswell turned to his second. 'Lieutenant Stanford, take the men and top out in the flat up there. I want a few moments to myself. I'll be up shortly.'

'Yes, sir.' Stanford turned to the line of cavalrymen ordering them to follow him. As the line of blue-clad troopers moved away, Captain Criswell watched them go, struggling with himself about this conflicting new information he'd suddenly received. He leaned back in the saddle, gazing higher, surrounded by the grandeur of ice-sheathed peaks dotted with tiny, greensward basins and silver rivulets twisting down below them. This vast mountain land seemed so quiet, so serene. Yet it was all a facade. The savage Crow Indians fighting to keep the white man out of their ancestral lands, the robberies, shooting and killings in towns and even out in wilderness areas, proved it was a wild and dangerous land no matter how beautiful it looked. This new possibility of changing orders only added to the confusion he had to deal with. If he decided to continue with his pursuit of the Crows, or turned back to New Hope, trying to pick up Keller's trail, he could be reprimanded or worse either way. Criswell pondered his dilemma until he had an idea that might cover both possibilities. Urging his horse forward he climbed the steep trail rejoining his men.

'Lieutenant, I want you ride for New Hope with ten men. Once you reach there send a rider on to Fort Jackson, with a message I'll write for them about why I've been forced, through new circumstances, to change my orders. If you can pick up this Keller gang's trail, stay with it if you believe you're closing in on them. Give yourself four or five days. If you can actually capture him, take him down to Fort Jackson. They'll likely hang him fast after all the misery he's caused the army. If you're unable to, ride back here and rejoin me fast as possible. I'll still be on the move so that will take you some time, and time is not on our side. I won't pretend not to be worried about engaging the Crow war party with only half my men, but I have no choice left to me. Get cracking, lieutenant!'

The fast ride out of New Hope, after the bank robbery, saw Cort, Red and Fan, each carrying a heavy sack of gold and silver in their saddle-bags. Cort, in the lead, kicked his horse south putting as much ground between New Hope, and Nate Whitman, as possible. Two weeks of steady riding brought the trio within sight of the first lower table lands and flat topped plateaus where mountains came down to meet this rugged new country carved with a thousand twisting canyons that led nowhere. Gone were lush meadows, icy peaks, the pungent aroma of tall pines. Instead they rode into an arid land of sagebrush and juniper jungles of Blackfoot country, deadly enemies of the Crows up north. Cort felt certain even Nate Whitman would not be able to follow them all the way down here. Even better neither he, Red or Fan, were known for what they were. They could move around out in the open with relative ease, riding into the few, widely scattered towns they came across without fear of being recognized. Reining to a stop at the end of an open plateau above Red Deer Canyon, the men saw a tiny cluster of buildings still far ahead.

'I could sure wet my whistle down there after eating all this dust,' Tyge said, licking dry lips.

'Yeah, and I wouldn't mind a real hot meal after eating all those stringy jackrabbits we've been eating,' Red chimed in. 'What about it, Cort? You want to ride down and have a look see?'

Keller didn't answer for several moments, intently studying the cluster of buildings with a thin pall of blue smoke hanging over them.

'Maybe, if we're careful,' his voice was cautionary. 'New Hope may be nearly three hundred miles away, but bad news travels fast and far.'

'There hasn't been any town we couldn't shoot our way out of yet,' Fan bragged. 'A hick town like that can't give us much trouble.'

'All right. Let's ride down and take a look. Remember, we're not here to draw any attention to ourselves. If there's any law there, that only brings more trouble. We brought plenty of both with us.'

The three men rode easily down the street eyeing each store front sign as they passed. By the end of the first block, Red already counted four saloons and two gambling houses. At the corner a bearded man crossed the street in front of them. Fan called out to him.

'Hey mister. This town got a name?'

'Sure we do. See all those whiskey dens you just rode past?'

'We did.'

'That's why we call it Whiskeytown. You could likely float a boat down main street on Saturday night, and you would-n't even need oars!' The man laughed, continuing on his way with a wave of his hand.

The second block matched the first with one notable exception. Half way down they saw a sign hanging over a door marked 'Sheriff's Office'. Cort looked to Red and Fan without saying anything. It was enough they knew a star man was here. At the end of the third block they saw the tall, pointed white steeple of a church with a wooden cross on top.

'At least this town ain't all bad,' Red nodded, eyeing the house of worship.

'All those sinners need a place to repent Sunday morning after what they did on Saturday night,' Fan mocked with a sly smile.

'You thinking about renting a room?' Red turned to his brother. 'I've sure had enough of sleeping out in the brush, haven't you?'

'Not yet,' Keller shook his head. 'I'm not ready to start rubbing shoulders with people we don't know. We've already seen they have a lawman here. Whether he's some hard-nosed type or just some local yokel to pin a badge on, we'll have to find out first. At least we can get a hot meal. That's something we all need. For the next few nights I still say we camp outside town. Let's take our time and look around here a while.'

Cort pushed through the door of the Cactus Flower diner, Red and Fan on his heels. The setting sun had blinked out behind black rock mesas, inviting the first glow of coal oil lamps lighting windows of saloons and gambling houses preparing for another night of risky business. Legitimate store owners had already closed their shops, locking doors, leaving for home before the usual rowdy crowd began filling the street. Once whiskey started flowing and gambling tables filled, the street would quickly turn into a free for all where nearly anything went and occasionally even bloody murder with smoking six-guns.

The small diner already had tables filled except for one over by the front window next to a big, pot bellied stove. Keller edged his way through men at tables until sitting down. Eaters shot a quick glance at the newcomers before going back to their vittles and conversations. A tall, skinny man in a grease-stained apron came up to the table. 'What'll be, gents?'

'You got a menu?' Fan asked.

'Yeah I do, right here in my head,' he pointed.

'All right, what are you cooking?'

'The special tonight is mule deer stew with some vegetables. If you want to go whole hog, I've got elk steaks with real potatoes, not those Indian roots some like to pass off as the real thing.'

'Give us the steaks,' Cort ordered.

'You mean all three of you?'

'That's what I mean.'

'You know you're talking about a forty-five dollar dinner, don't you?'

'I'm not worried about the price. Just get it on the table hot. Bring us a pot of coffee, too.'

The greasy apron started back across the room humming with conversation, while Cort sat back eyeing the crowd of men at tables around them. It felt good to be out of the saddle after the long ride, and even better Nate Whitman wasn't breathing down the back of their necks. He hoped it might be possible to stay around town a while and give all three men a rest. From somewhere up the street the jangling sound of rinky-tinky piano music began as

Whiskeytown opened up for another night of non-stop drinking and gambling. Dinner came with all three eagerly digging into the hot, juicy provender. As they ate the front door opened. In stepped an older man wearing a tin star. Cort had his back to the door. Fan, sitting opposite Keller, quickly nudged him under the table.

'Look what just came in,' he nodded over Cort's shoulder, Keller twisting in the seat.

'Just keep eating,' he whispered, pouring himself another cup of coffee.

Loyal Horton stood for a moment looking the crowded room over for a seat. The only empty one he saw was at Keller's table. He crossed the room with a nod here and a hello there from diners who knew him until he stood looking down at the three men.

'You've got the only empty chair in the house. Mind if I sit down and fill it?'

'Help yourself.' Cort glanced up, Red stiffening beside him, Fan's hand slowly moving down to his six-gun until Cort made the slightest gesture with his head stopping him.

'I know most everyone in town. I don't recollect seeing you three before.'

'We're just passing through.' Cort kept it short, continuing to eat and trying to ignore the lawman.

Horton looked like he'd lived every day of his forty-nine years. His wrinkled, deeply-tanned face sprouted grey whiskers and sideburns under a well-worn Stetson hat. The star was pinned on a sagging shirt that said he was mostly skin and bones. He didn't look like much of a sheriff but more a figurehead, someone to pin a badge on, while the rowdy citizens of Whiskeytown cut loose doing pretty much as they wanted. Horton noticed the steaks his silent guests were busily eating.

'You boys must be doing pretty well, to order up something like that,' he questioned without getting a response, as the cookie came back to the table.

'What'll you have, Loyal?'

'I can't afford those streaks, so I guess its venison stew for me. Bring me a cup of coffee too, Lenny.'

The sheriff eyed his strangely silent guests trying another question. 'Where you boys from?'

Keller looked up, already edgy of the verbal sparing. 'Nowhere, really. We're just on the move wherever another job shows up. We're here today and next week a hundred miles away.'

'I understand that. There's a lot of men today doing pretty much the same thing especially since the war over the South ended. Did I catch just a hint of southern twang in your voice?'

Cort stopped eating. Red and Fan didn't look up, growing more apprehensive with each question. 'My family lived in Tennessee. That could be what you hear. Being from the South isn't a crime yet, is it?'

'No, no it sure isn't, especially out here in the west. We didn't get much involved in it. This is different country with different people, if you know what I mean.'

'It is different.' Cort finished off his last bite of steak, Red and Fan wolfing down theirs so they could get up and leave without any more questions.

'Here's your venison stew, Loyal,' Lenny came back to the table. 'If you want seconds, I can try to fish you out a little bit more meat.'

The sheriff didn't answer, watching the three men get to their feet. 'Nice talking to you. Enjoy Whiskeytown. There's lots to see and do so long as you don't get yourself in any kind of real trouble.'

He watched the trio edge their way back across the room until Cort paid for dinner and they exited the Cactus Flower.

Loyal Horton might not look or act like much of a real lawman like Nate Whitman, but he did have a sheriff's instincts of curiosity and suspicion after all the years he'd worn the badge. His three tablemates had said little as possible. It made him wonder why. Were they hiding something, or just not the friendly type. All three seemed to have a quiet kind of tension just under the surface ready to explode if the wrong thing was said or question asked. He'd remember these three if they stayed around town very long. Maybe going over the wanted posters back in his office wouldn't be a bad idea either.

Once outside on the street, Red was first to speak. 'That tin star liked to ask too many questions. I don't care how old and worn out he looked.'

'You think he might be trouble, Cort?' Fan asked as they kept walking. Keller didn't answer for several seconds. When he did it was short and to the point.

'He's just like the rest of that breed. Always smelling around for something.'

'I'd kind of like to stick around here a while longer,' Fan replied. 'This town is wide open and we could use a little fun for once after all the time and miles it took us to get here. What do you say to it, Cort?'

'I think we can if we're careful. That's the closest a badge has gotten to me in a long time, even if he doesn't know who we are. I agree we could use a little rest, and so can our horses. I ran them pretty hard, but I had to. If we are going to lay low I've got another idea.'

'What's that?' Red questioned.

'I'd like to put all the cash we're carrying someplace safer than our saddle-bags or camp.'

'Where else is there?" Tyge wondered.

'Like the bank we saw when we rode in.'

'A bank? Banks get robbed . . . by men like us,' Tyge challenged the idea.

'How could we do that without drawing more suspicion to ourselves?' Red's tone made it clear he didn't think much of his brother's suggestion either.

'I don't mean to deposit all of it. About half would be better. We can hold on to the rest of it, then go into the bank one at a time on different days. If anyone does get nosey, we can say we're looking to buy property and run some cattle. Take a look around us. Money is flowing everyplace you look. The saloons and gambling parlors are open day and night filled with men spending money. The bank has to be used to seeing plenty of hard cash from businesses too, going in and out. I don't think anyone is going to pay much attention to us making deposits. Even if we only stay here a couple of weeks, I say the bank is the safest place to put our cash.'

Red shook his head, a small smile creasing his whiskered face. Leave it up to his brother to come up with an idea like this. If there was one thing he could always count on, it was that Cort would have ideas no one else would. That had to be the main reason how they'd been able to stay free on the run, never getting caught. It was the same thinking back home that kept them off the Union Army gallows, when they were still just wild, young teenagers. Now they were even outrunning the United States Cavalry, for the same reasons. If Cort thought it was a good idea to put their cash in the bank, he'd go along with it. Why bet against the success they'd had over these last eight years.

The sun was well up and the streets of Whiskeytown, at nine o'clock in the morning, were nearly deserted. Cort, Red and Fan sat in their saddles in front of the Mesalands Bank & Trust, waiting for it to open. Cort pulled up his pocket watch. 'They should open in a few minutes, if they're on time.'

61

'Know what?' Fan said shaking his head. 'This is the first time I ever went into a bank to put money in instead of taking it out at gun point. It feels kind of funny.'

Red laughed under his breath. 'Yeah, it is something different for sure.'

Shades went up on windows and the front door. An older man wearing a dark suit keyed the lock, opening the door and inviting his early customers inside. Cort was first up to one of the two teller cages. His brother and Tyge flanked him to see how to deposit their cash. A second man entered the bank as Cort began writing. The bank manager got up from his desk, coming to the second cage standing alongside the teller.

'Good morning, Mr Sheldon. You're in early. Must have had a big night, huh?'

'We did indeed, Jeffery. Did you hear about that bad business up north?'

'Up north? No, what about it?'

Cort stopped writing. Anything about the country they'd run from might be worth listening to.

'I had a customer last night just down from there. He says some marshal named Whitman killed a couple of men from this Keller gang, that's been making the papers. They robbed an Army pay roll, and a bank in town too. One was posing as a rancher somewhere near Janesville. The second man was wounded, hiding out at an old mine not far from New Hope. I imagine a marshal like that means real business. We could sure use someone like that around here, instead of you know who.'

Cort's hand suddenly clenched the pencil, breaking it in two, crushing the deposit slip in his hand and starting for the front door. The bank manager called after him.

'I can take care of you, gentlemen. No need to rush off.'

Once outside, Red and Fan drew close fearing Keller

might explode with rage. Red put both hands firmly on his brother's shoulders, locking eyes with him. Before he could speak, Cort cut him off.

'I'm riding back to New Hope, to kill Whitman!'

Red pulled him closer. 'You can't do that. That's exactly what Whitman wants. He can't find us, so this is his way of drawing you in. Don't take the bait. We'll kill him in due time. But let's do it our way when we call the time and place, not him. Wic and Coy were close friends and blood kin to me, too. Don't think I don't want to settle that score just as much as you do. But this is one time you better listen to me, baby brother. We both want the same thing. Let's do it together whether it's two months or two years from now. It will get done, and I'll be right there with you. So will Fan. I promise you that. I'll swear to it on Mom's bible.'

CHAPTER SIX

Lieutenant Martin Stanford led his men into New Hope, ramrod straight and square jawed, proudly projecting the prestige and image of the United States Cavalry. This was the very first time he'd been given command completely on his own. He had his orders from Captain Criswell, and meant to carry them out to every letter of military law. The first order of business was to send one of his men riding fast down to Fort Jackson, with Criswell's message. Sending the trooper on his way, he found Sergeant O'Halloran laying on a cot, face down in the marshal's office, still suffering from the gaping bullet wound that had raked across his back. The sergeant wasn't surprised to see the young officer.

'I figured Criswell would send someone when my rider reached him. I didn't think he'd send you with ten men, though,' he grimaced as he spoke.

'What about this Keller bunch? Did you learn anything about them before you were wounded?'

'Yeah, they're stone cold killers. They shot me and Whitman's deputy down without a call, killing him. They're a bunch of southern rebels who think they're still fighting the war. Whitman is the expert on all of them. He's tangled with them before. He even killed one of their cousins that was hiding them over near Janesville, and another gang member who was wounded out in an old mine outside of town here. He's the one you want to talk to, if you've got orders to go after them.'

'Where's he at now, do you know?'

'Here in town someplace. Probably making the rounds himself since he doesn't have a deputy anymore. He's easy to spot. Stands over six feet tall and wears a wide brimmed tan Stetson.'

'Is there some way you can get down to Fort Jackson, and have a military doctor take a look at your back wound?'

'Not likely. I can't ride like this. I'm full of stitches. Every time I even draw a breath it feels like I'm being torn apart. Unless someone wants to take me in a wagon where I can lay down, I'm not going anyplace.'

'From what you've said this marshal sounds like the man to talk to. You rest easy while I try to find him.'

'I wish I could get up off this cot and go with you when you ride out. I've got a lot to get even over. I want to see that whole bunch howling in hell with the devil. Even that's too good for those Johnny Rebs!'

Marshal Whitman and his Crow sidekick stood talking on the street to the owner of Hinky's Brass Rail saloon, when Lieutenant Stanford walked up introducing himself.

Whitman looked the young cavalry officer up and down sizing him up, while Sanford explained his reason for being in town.

When he finished, Whitman commented, 'The cavalry is sending you and who else after Keller?' His tone already made it clear he thought the whole idea was pure folly.

'Me and my men, sir. I've had them bivouac just outside town until I get the information I need from you.'

'Do you have any idea where you're going to start

running him down?'

'No sir, not yet. I was told you could help me with that information. Captain Criswell ordered me to look you up when I got into town. I'm following those orders.'

'I don't know who this Captain Criswell of yours is, but just because he thinks all this is simple as that, tells me he doesn't have any idea what he's talking about. If I knew where Keller is I wouldn't be standing here talking to you, I'd be out after him myself. Him and that bunch of killers who run with him could be anywhere by now. I've already killed two of his men. I've got at least three more to go. You ought to take your soldier boys and ride back to your captain and tell him Keller could be a thousand miles away by now. You'd also save yourself a lot of boot leather riding all over the country for nothing.'

'I can't do that, sir. Captain Criswell has given me my orders. I have to try to carry them out. I'm sure you can understand that.'

Whitman was already getting tired of the conversation. He stared back at the young lieutenant, his impatience rising. 'I don't care if Ulysses S. Grant told you to go after Keller. I'm telling you it's a waste of time. No one right now knows where he might be. I've got Crow friends of mine out looking for him. Until I get some solid information like that, there's no sense riding off anywhere. Do I make myself clear?'

Stanford stood dumbstruck with the rank disrespect the law man showed for the military he loved so much. Even worse were his remarks about General Grant, his personal hero. He struggled to respond. 'At least . . . if you won't help me, will you even suggest what general direction Keller might have gone?'

'If you insist on an answer I'll give you a simple one. He can be anyplace between here and the Mexican order. Does that give you enough ground to start out on, lieutenant?'

Little Hawk stood at Whitman's side without uttering a word. There were few white men he'd normally speak to or tolerate. His hate for the cavalry that had waged an incessant war against his people made him look upon the young officer as a bitter enemy never to be trusted or helped in any way. Stanford saw that hate in his dark eyes, avoiding his penetrating stare.

'I've been given a week by Captain Criswell, to try and pick up the gang's trail. I won't waste any more time here in New Hope. I had hoped we could join forces to go after this bunch together. You've made it quite clear that isn't going to be the case. I'll bid you good day, Marshal.' Stanford saluted smartly and started back up the street as Whitman watched him go slowly shaking his head.

'Those poor fools have no ideal what they're doing. They'll never catch Keller with some cavalry patrol. They come riding in here all high and mighty like they think they can demand anything they want because they ride in here with flag flying and fancy uniforms. Cort Keller is too smart for them and the rest of the government too. I'm the one who's going to end his career. I know more about him and how he thinks than any regiment of cavalry ever will, and I'll prove it to all of them one way or the other.'

The setting sun lost itself behind slanted, black rock mesas, while Cort sat lost in thought in the small camp the three men had made several miles outside of Whiskeytown.

Red and Tyge glanced at each other without saying a word. They knew Cort was suffering in silence over the killings of his cousin and Wic, at the hands of Nate Whitman's bloody badge. The smoldering hate Cort felt wouldn't burn itself out until he faced the marshal man to man, gunning him down, no matter what it cost him.

67

Red lifted the boiling coffee pot from the fire, pouring himself a cup and one for Fan too. Looking to his brother, he wondered if he should break the silence. He decided to take the chance. 'Coffee's hot. You want a cup, Cort?'

Keller broke his stare straightening up with a barely audible sigh. 'Yeah, Red, I'll have one.' He reached for the steaming cup. 'And I want to thank you for talking some sense into me back at the bank. I guess I lost my head for a few minutes. Coy and Wic gone makes me wonder if sometimes we all wouldn't have been better off to stay back in Tennessee, and ride out the bad times. Those two men were like brothers to me, as close as you are to me. I still can't believe they're both dead.'

'I know how you feel. I feel the same way myself. We'll get Whitman, somewhere, some time. Just not right now. I know your hurt, kinda made you crazy for a few minutes. I'm just glad I was there to stop you.'

'So am I.'

'What's next for us?' Tyge wondered.

'I still want to deposit some of our money in the bank.' Cort answered. 'We'll go in tomorrow and get it done this time.'

'I figured we'd do that, but what about afterwards? Are we going to stick around for a while or pull up stakes in a week and ride out?'

'We've got plenty of cash, so we don't need another job, at least not right now. You said you wanted to spend some time in town enjoying yourself, so we can lay low for a while. We're far enough south we can rest a while instead of always being on the run.'

'What about you two? You going to join me?' Fan questioned.

'You and Red go in if you like. I'm not as big at it as you two are. You can cut the dog loose as long as you don't cause any trouble. Just remember not to draw any attention to yourselves. We don't need that.'

'Me, draw attention to myself?' The sly grin on Fan's face made it clear he thought the comment was almost funny. 'What about you, Red? You going to join me for a little drink and maybe a dance with some pretty lady? You remember ladies, don't you? They're sort of soft and smell good?'

'I might if Cort doesn't mind staying out here alone.' He looked to his brother for an answer.

'I don't. You two go ahead. Only be careful.'

The streets of Whiskeytown were already crowded with dark figures going in and out of bars and gambling dens, when Red and Tyge pulled their horses to a halt in front of the Red Eye saloon. From somewhere up the street the jangling sound of banjo music could be heard. The two men tied their horses off at the hitching rail before pushing through the door into the Red Eye, taking in the scene. A single large room had a long mahogany bar along one wall opposite tables filled with drinkers talking loudly. At the far end a small, elevated stage stood empty. In one corner right of the stage, a bald-headed man sat at a piano tickling the keys, warming up his fingers for another night of shouted requests.

'Lively joint, ain't it?' Fan turned to Red with a smile on his face, working his way up to the bar. A burly man with hair parted straight down the middle came up behind the counter.

'What's your poison, gents?'

'Give us a couple of whiskeys,' Tyge said, the bar man pulling up a bottle and two stubby glasses, filling them to the brim.

'That'll be five dollars,' he said.

'Five dollars for two whiskeys?' Fan questioned.

'That's it, mister. This is the genuine article, Old Stump Blower. Not that swill other saloons pour watered down with creosote oil. Take it or leave it.'

Fan pushed a shiny, five dollar gold coin across the counter still eyeing the man skeptically, as he turned away to other customers.

'Maybe I should buy the whole bottle, and not get five dollared to death,' Fan mocked.

'No, I don't think that's a good idea. We don't want to get drunk. Remember what Cort said?'

'Yeah, I know. But after that long ride down here from up north, we've got to cut loose and have a little fun, don't we?'

'Damn little. When the whiskey starts talking trouble is right behind it. If we want to stay around town for a while we'd better keep that in mind. Let's get to a table and sit down. I don't want to prop up this bar all night.'

The pair made their way across the noisy room to sit at a small table next to the piano player. Tyge ordered two more whiskeys chasing the first pair down. The piano man began playing an upbeat tune without singing words to it. Tyge listened a moment before turning toward him.

'What's the name of that song? I've never heard it before.'

'They call it Marching Through Georgia. It's a new military song very popular back east. I was lucky to get the sheet music to it.'

'Who is suppose to be marching through Georgia, the boys in grey?'

'No, the Union Army. You know, Sherman's march to the sea.'

'That's a Yankee lie. Play something else. I don't want to hear any more of it!'

'But it's brand new. Everyone likes it.'

'I don't care what everyone likes. I don't. Play something else.'

'Like what?'

'You know Dixie Land, don't you?'

The piano man stopped playing. A pained look came over his face.

'Well, don't you?' Fan insisted.

'Yes, I now it . . . but.'

'I don't want to hear any "buts" about it. I said play it.'

The piano man turned back to the keyboard, lightly fingering the opening notes to Dixie Land.

'Play it louder. I can't hear it over all this noise,' Fan demanded, his patience growing short.

Red reached over grabbing Tyge's arm pulling him close. 'Let it go. It's not worth arguing over.'

'I don't care. I want to hear it." He tipped up his glass, draining it in one fast gulp.

A man several tables away shouted at the piano man. 'Hey, what's the slop you're playing? Play something else. This ain't Atlanta!'

Fan immediately rose to his feet, glaring at the stranger. 'You keep right on playing it,' he ordered the piano man.

At that moment Loyal Horton came through the door into the Red Eye. Keller saw him first, ordering Fan to sit down and shut up, but the whiskey was already doing the talking. He ignored Red's plea.

'We don't want to hear any of that Confederate slop!' The stranger got up from his chair, pointing a finger at Fan. 'And if you don't like it, go someplace else!'

'You're a yellow dog Yankee!' Fan shouted back. Red tried to grab his arm but he shoved him away. Taking a step away from the table, Tyge cleared his gun holster for action.

Men at tables between the pair scrambled to get out of the way, clearing an opening. Horton saw what was coming, pushing through tables and starting across the room before a gunfight broke out. The piano man jumped off his stool, diving around behind the piano for cover.

'I said you're a yellow dog Yankee. What are you going to do about it, big mouth!'

'You're nothing but southern trash. You lost the war. Now you're gonna lose in here too!'

The stranger stabbed for his pistol, but he never had a prayer. Fan's .44 cleared the holster spitting flame and hot lead once, twice, before the man could even thumb back the hammer on his six-gun. Bullet impacts drove him back through surrounding tables until he crashed to the floor quivering in death.

'Hold it right there and drop that gun. I don't want two killings in here the same night!' Horton stood only ten feet way leveling his six-gun on Fan. 'Do it now or so help me I'll drop you!'

Tyge spun facing the lawman, the .44 still firm in his hands. He had three more 220 grain lead bullets snug in their chambers. All he had to do was pull the trigger, and Horton would be a dead man.

'Don't shoot, Tyge!' Red jumped to his feet and stepped between the two men. 'We've got a lot more at stake here than some big mouth. Give me the gun. We'll get through this without any more killing.'

Fan hesitated, still gripping the big Colt, his eyes fixed on Horton. 'I'm not going to any jail. Not for this two bit star man or anyone else!'

'No one said you would. Just give me the gun before it gets any worse. Everyone here saw what happened. It was a fair fight. He meant to pull on you too.'

'You better tell your friend to hand over that pistol, and I mean right now!'

Fan's crazed stare went from Red to the sheriff and back

again. Red extended his hand talking nearly as a whisper. 'Let it go. We don't need any more trouble. Remember what Cort said. Give me the gun. I'll stand up for you no matter what. If you pull that trigger we're on the run again.'

Tyge's didn't move a muscle for several seconds longer until Red's hand gripped the six-gun, slowly pulling it away. 'You better be right on this Red.' His voice was tense with emotion.

'I am. You'll see. Let's end this right now.'

'You two will have to come with me over to my office.' Horton said, before turning to men around him ordering them to carry out the body. 'Let's go.'

Sheriff Horton unlocked the door to his office motioning Red and Fan to step inside. Tossing the keys atop his desk, he sat in the swivel chair eyeing both men before saying anything. He had a killing to deal with and was trying to think of how to be stern yet not force another gun fight. He motioned the men to sit in chairs opposite his desk.

'Listen, you two. This town didn't get its name by drawing straws out of a hat. There's good reason why it's called Whiskeytown. It's not Abilene Kansas, with two hundred whiskey-starved droves and two thousand head of long horns being driven in each month raising hell, either. I don't need that kind of trouble or what you started with this shooting. I let a lot of little things go on but there's a limit to how much I'll put up with. Everyone here knows Lard Bullard was a big mouth trouble maker, and they probably knew one day he'd end up calling out the wrong man. He tried to draw first. I saw that. But I can't have strangers come riding in here gunning down citizens. Do you both understand what I'm saying? I'm not some hell for leather shotgun sheriff, but if you two promise you'll keep your guns holstered and no more of what happened at the Red Eye, I'll let you two walk out of here without any jail time. One other thing. I want your names. What do you say to it?'

Thinking fast Red nodded with a quick answer. 'Yeah, we understand. We didn't ride in here looking for trouble. It just happened like you saw. My name is Joe Brown. My friend here is Dade Wilson.'

'What about the other man, the one I saw with you at the diner?'

'He's John Morgan. We all travel together looking for work. We thought Whiskeytown might be a good place to start.'

'All right. I'll write them down. Just remember what I said about all this.'

'We sure will. You don't have to worry about that. Let's go, Dade.' The pair got to their feet along with Horton, reaching across the desk shaking hands.

'I'm glad we understand each other. It makes my job a whole lot easier.' He watched the pair walk out the door before sitting down to ink the names on a piece of paper, slipping it into the desk drawer.

Cort heard horses coming into camp. Getting to his feet he stepped away from the flickering fire, hand on his six-gun just in case. Peering into the dark he heard his brother's high, three note signal whistle. A moment later Red and Fan rode out of the dark into the circle of light.

'You two are back early,' Cort said surprised.

'Yeah, we are,' Red nodded. 'We sorta didn't have any choice.'

'What do you mean by that?' Cort's voice was more concerned than the question sounded.

'Ah, we had a little trouble back in town.'

'Like what?'

Red glanced at Fan who knelt next to the fire pouring

himself a cup of hot coffee. 'Go head, tell him Red,' Fan offered.

'Well . . . this drunk in the Red Eye called Tyge out. He had to make a move to stand his ground. He couldn't let that whiskey breath buffalo him in front of everyone . . . could he?'

'You mean gunplay? Don't tell me you let that happen after what I warned you two about before you left here.'

'This guy just pushed it. What were we suppose to do, sit there and take it? You wouldn't have. I know that for sure.'

'Damnit, Red! Now we'll have to pack it up and run for it again.'

'No, we won't. We had a talk with Horton, the sheriff. He saw it all himself. He said that whiskey breath was a trouble maker who had it coming to him. If it wasn't Tyge who took him down it would have been someone else. By the way, while I'm talking about it your new name is John Morgan.'

'What are you talking about?'

'Horton wanted our names after the shoot out, so I made up three real quick while we were in his office. That way if there's any paper on us none of them will match up.'

Cort stood shaking his head in dismay. 'We don't need any of this. You both know that don't you?'

'It just happened,' Fan finally spoke up. 'I didn't go in there looking for trouble. I think Red got us in the clear over it. He's such a good liar he's just about got me believing my name is Dade Wilson. He was real smooth about it. We'll be all right.'

Keller stared back at both men. The look on his face said he couldn't understand how both men actually thought the sheriff would forget about the killing and buy Red's wild story. 'You both believe Horton is that dumb? Is that what you're telling me after I warned both of you not to make any trouble?'

Fan was getting tired of the tongue lashing. He stood up glaring at Cort. 'I didn't have any selection in it. Why can't you understand that? It was him or me. Just that simple. Horton saw it. He let us walk, didn't he? Why beat it to death?'

Cort turned back to the fire pit cussing under his breath. He had enough to worry about and now this on top of it. The killing had to spell trouble despite Red's fast thinking. Sooner of later he knew it would work against them. The only thing he was sure of now was that it was too late to do anything about it.

CHAPTER SEVEN

A whiskey-colored sunrise rose over its namesake town spotlighting Loyal Horton keying the lock on the front door of his office stepping inside. He'd spent part of the previous night troubled about Bullard's killing. The lightning fast way of Dade Wilson's gun handling still bothered him. Wilson was no cow puncher or saddle bum. Not the way he moved with a six-gun in his hand. His friend Joe Brown was a fast talker almost too willing to cooperate with him. The third man in the trio he'd only met briefly at the Cactus Flower, had barely spoken two words during their brief encounter. When he added all three up there was something about them that didn't seem to make sense. Was there something more, or was it just his natural suspicion of strangers that kept him asking so many questions of himself.

He sat in his swivel chair pulling at his chin thinking all this over. Opening a desk drawer he took out a small stack of wrinkled wanted posters, beginning to slowly thumb through them one by one. He'd never paid much attention to them in the past but now his curiosity changed that. Near the bottom he came to a recent one he'd tossed in the drawer without a second look. What made it so unusual was it was a government issued poster. He'd never seen one quite like it before. Bold black letters at the top shouted REWARD. $5,000. WANTED DEAD OR ALIVE. Below was a rough description and drawing of four men and their suspected names, chronicling the holdup of a US Government payroll wagon somewhere near New Hope, on May 5th 1867. It ordered anyone knowing the whereabouts of the men to contact either the nearest Cavalry Post, or Marshal Nathaniel Whitman, in New Hope.

Horton slid the poster back atop the desk. Leaning back in the squeaky chair he closed his eyes rubbing the kinks out of his neck, thinking all this over. Joe Brown had given him his name quick enough and the other two men. None of them matched the names on this poster, and it also said there were four holdup men. Brown and his friends were only three. He argued with himself whether he was letting his imagination get the best of him or whether he should go ahead and try to do something about it. He finally reached into a drawer, pulling out writing paper and began a letter to Marshal Whitman, in New Hope. He knew it was a long shot and might all be a wild goose chase, but he was a lawman after all even if not of the hell for leather firebrand.

Twenty miles outside of Whiskeytown, Many Horses, one of the Indian scouts Nate Whitman had put the word out to try and track down the Keller gang, pulled his paint pony to a stop. His dark eyes had been following the trail of three riders for over two weeks, winding south in and out road-less canyons, dry creek beds, leaving cold fire pits in their wake. Each day of his careful tracking he'd grown more certain the men he followed did not want to be found because of the back country way they traveled avoiding common roads and even rough trails. Many Horses turned to the pair of dark-skinned braves riding with him, Wolf Runs and Buffalo Shield.

'These white eyes are riding for "noisy village" ahead. I will stay on their tracks. You ride for Whitman. Tell him I want four good horses with shoes, for this information. Ride fast. I do not want to follow them farther south into the land of our enemy, the Cheyenne. Tell him come quick.'

The pair of scouts galloped off into brush leaving Many Horses riding slowly ahead, eyes still glued to the ground. New Hope lay nearly two weeks behind them. Because the slow work of tracking was no longer needed for Wolf Runs and Buffalo Shield, they could ride flat-out cutting that time down to eight or nine days. Many Horses could now make better time too. He was certain he knew where the dim hoof prints would lead, to the only white man's town in these endless mesa lands. He'd been there once before but only to see how the white men lived and drink some of their potent fire water. The constant mix of noise, music and loud men both day and night, made it someplace he could not stay long. The white men were like so many ants always talking, shouting, always on the move. He would never understand how they could live the way they did.

Cort sat in camp discussing whether to pack up and leave Whiskeytown, or take the chance to stay longer. Especially cautious after Fan's killing in the Red Eye, he was still unsure, but made his opinion known.

'I think we're all right,' Tyge countered. 'Horton bought what Red told him. Every single word of it. I'm for staying at least a little while longer. New Hope is way up north. No one down here can make any connection to us there.'

'What about you, Red?' Cort asked.

'I guess I'd like to stay a while longer too. South of here is Colorado Territory, and Indian country. Whitman is bad enough without taking on the Cheyenne, too. This might be the last place where we can take a break before going back to eating jackrabbit and rattlesnake. But you have to know I'll go along with whatever you decide, if it comes down to that.'

Cort stared into the dancing fire pit flames without answering for several minutes, trying to make a final decision. He relied on Red's judgment as much as his brother did his, yet hesitated even while answering.

'I know both of you want to take it easy and give the horses a good feed and break from all the traveling. I'm still worried about staying here after the shoot out. It had to get Horton's attention. I'm sure of that. I'm leery about what he might do or who he might try to contact. I say if we stay a while longer we'll have to walk light and keep our eyes open. Another week is about all I'll go for. After that we should pack up and ride out of here.'

'What if Horton actually did try to do something?' Fan spoke up again. 'He wouldn't stand a chance against any of us in a shoot out. I saw that about him right off. He's not going to face anyone down one on one. I wouldn't worry much about him.'

'Maybe,' Cort countered. 'But if he got help that could change things fast.'

'Help, from who, where?' Fan wouldn't let it go.

'I'm not sure yet. If he did get curious enough about us he might ask for some. The cavalry must come through here from time to time with all the Indian attacks they have to deal with. I'm not sure how much law is south of here, but there must be other towns, they could have star men too.'

Red nodded in agreement before a suggestion. 'Why don't we lay low here and take it easy for another week. That way when we do ride out we'll have fresh horses and we'll be ready too?'

'All right. But no more gun play,' Cort agreed. 'We can't afford to get involved in that again. You both understand me?'

Red nodded, while Tyge stirred the fire with a stick without answering. He wondered to himself if Keller was getting soft. As far as he was concerned he had no problem pulling his six-gun to settle any problem with anyone. The gang had made their reputation doing exactly that. Why the sudden change now? All this talk of being careful and cautious, tip toeing around town sounded almost laughable to him. Even worse, it could be dangerous to all three of them. He decided then and there he'd take care of himself no matter what Cort or his brother said. He'd learned that lesson early on when he was only thirteen years old, killing the man his mother lived with with a shotgun, after he'd continually beaten her when he was drunk. He also learned that killing came easy if you were first to pull the trigger. That single credo had guided all his adult life. He wasn't worried about Horton or anyone else he could bring in to help him. Tyge Fan would drop all of them before they could even blink.

Lieutenant Stanford had used up his one week up north trying to pick up the trail of the Keller gang. Exactly as Nat Whitmore had rudely predicted, nothing had come of all his efforts. He and his men had wandered south of New Hope for over thirty miles and not found a single track. His orders from Captain Criswell were to return to the main troop when that time was up and continue to try and engage the renegade Crow war party Criswell had been pursuing deep into their mountain stronghold. Stanford's return trip took him back near New Hope. Even though he had no interest seeing the marshal again, he did want to see Sergeant O'Halloran and how he was doing recovering from his bullet wound. Arriving in town late in the afternoon he had his men stable their horses in the livery for a good feed before walking to the marshal's office hoping Whitman would not be there. Pushing through the door the first thing he saw was Whitman sitting at his desk.

'What are you doing back here in town, Lieutenant?' A surprised look came over the marshal's face.

'I've used up my allotted time trying to find some sign of the Keller gang. I have to return to Captain Criswell's command. I stopped here to see how Sergeant O'Halloran was doing.'

'He's gone. Left here a week ago for Fort Jackson, when he felt good enough to ride again. You better turn your men around and head there too.'

'Why would that be? I have my orders from the captain.'

'Haven't the scouts from Jackson found you yet with the message?'

'No, what message?'

'Your captain and most of his men were ambushed by the Crows, up in Volcano Butte country. Most of them were killed including Criswell. A few stragglers made it back here to town with the story. They said they never had a chance. Criswell led them right into an ambush. He was killed in the first volley of shots.'

Stanford stood dumbfounded unable to speak. He took a few halting steps forward, slowly lowering himself into a chair opposite the desk, never taking his eyes off Whitman. 'Are you. . . certain of all this?'

'As certain as the men who came back here to tell it, wounded and bloody.'

The lieutenant slowly shook his head in stunned disbelief. The slaughter of Criswell and his friends with him was more than he could imagine. Criswell might not be the friendliest officer he'd ever known, but to be killed like this was nearly inconceivable. He swallowed hard taking a deep breath before finally speaking.

'I'll have to . . . take my men and start for Fort Jackson as quick as I can.'

'Wait just a minute, lieutenant. I've got another idea. How far south did you say you rode looking for Keller?'

'Maybe . . . thirty miles or so. Why?'

'Because if you're riding south, I just might join you. If Keller is anyplace my bet is he's farther down in mesa country someplace. We might turn that bad luck of yours around yet. Remember, I'm still looking for him, too. I've got a personal score to settle with him outside of this badge. I'll deputize a couple of men to look after things while we're gone. We're both going on this ride together, lieutenant!'

Sun-up next morning was barely one hour old when Marshal Whitman and Little Hawk eased into saddles next to Stanford and his disheveled looking line of troopers, deprived of the rest in town they'd been promised. Whitman eyed the raggedy looking men in blue.

'You and your men ready, lieutenant? They look a little worn, to me.'

'They'll follow my orders. Don't you worry about that, sir.'

'Good. Once they get a brace of fresh air in their lungs, and Little Hawk finds a trail worth following, I expect they'll buck up quick and show the real soldier boys they are. It's time we get down to some real tracking instead of riding all over the country wasting time wearing everyone out achieving nothing.'

Stanford didn't answer this time. The insult was clear enough without haggling over it.

The odd band of US Marshal, Indian tracker and small

line of cavalrymen traveled south three days before Little Hawk reined to a stop near high noon, pointing ahead at the figure of two riders coming fast towards them. He turned to Whitman with a single word. 'Indians.'

'Are they hostiles?' Stanford was immediately on the alert. 'Should I make my men ready?'

'No. Don't be foolish,' Whitman scolded. 'They're part of the scouting party I sent out to see if they could pick up Keller's trail. The way they're moving they must have something to tell me.'

Wolf Runs and Buffalo Shield pulled their sweaty horses to a dusty stop. Little Hawk immediately engaged them talking in their own tongue. It only took a moment to relay their message to Whitman.

'Many Horses rides four days away. He says the men we want are riding for "noisy village". He wants four horses with shoes for telling you this.'

'Noisy village, what's that?' Whitman questioned.

'Many Horses does not know its name. Only that many white men lived there.'

Lieutenant Stanford suddenly spoke up. 'The only town that far ahead could be Whiskeytown. It's about twenty-five miles west of Fort Jackson. I've never been there but I have heard a lot about it from enlisted men who have when I was stationed at the fort two years ago. It's full of lots of gambling, drinking and women.'

'Sounds like exactly the kind of place Keller and his bunch would head for. They'd mix right in. You tell these two we'll follow them back to Many Horses. And tell them he'll only get his horses when I find out if Keller is actually there!'

'Wait a minute, marshal. You have to understand me and my men cannot accompany you all the way to Whiskeytown, don't you?' Stanford said.

'And why not? I'll need you to take Keller down.'

'My orders from Captain Criswell were to only spend a week or so trying to track down Keller. That time is up. I have to report back to command at Fort Jackson.'

'No you don't. Criswell is dead and so are the orders he gave you. You want to make a name for yourself, don't you? Bringing in Cort Keller is the way to do that. We can both ride for the fort after we take him dead or alive. It makes no difference to me which way. That's how you make captain, lieutenant. Do you understand what I'm saying?'

The young officer sat in the saddle staring back without a quick answer. Maybe Whitman was correct. Maybe things could all work out exactly that way. He could almost visualize himself riding at the head of a line into the fort with Keller and his men roped together behind him. What a sight that would be!

'I'll ride with you. . . at least until another few days.' He finally got the words out. 'Then see what happens.'

Jeff Banks sat at Nate Whitman's office desk back in New Hope, reading a letter just delivered. Both he and his pal Wayne Little had been deputized by Whitman to keep an eye on things around town while the marshal was gone. Finishing the letter he sat back looking across the small office at Little. 'This letter is some kind of trouble,' he said.

'What kind of trouble?'

'It's from a sheriff down in Whiskeytown, way south of here. He asked about three men that showed up there he thinks could be on the run from the law. He wants Nate to see if he knows anything about them, but he's already gone. What do we do about it now?'

Little shrugged. He had no answer either. 'He's been gone what, three or four days now? I can't saddle up and catch up to him. I don't even know where he's going or how far?'

'Maybe I could write back and tell him all this but what good would that do? He wants Nate to talk to him not me.'

'It might be best to let it go until Nate comes back. He'll be able to help him. I know we sure can't. We aren't really deputies, are we?'

'Makes sense to me. I'll put the letter right here under the ink well so we don't forget it and he can't miss it either.'

Cort had put the limit on their stay in Whiskeytown, no longer than one more week. Four of those days had already passed. He was ready to withdraw the money he'd earlier put in the bank and buy supplies for the trail. He wasn't sure yet exactly where they'd go, only that it would be some-place farther south. That land should be wild and unpeopled except for Indians, and they don't carry badges. All three men were in town at Hanson's Dry Goods & Hardware store as Cort went down the list of items to buy. Adam Hanson the owner, stood behind the counter talking to Cort.

'You men must be leaving town with a long list like that,' he smiled back.

'We'll be on the move,' Cort acknowledged but nothing more. 'Can you fill all of this?' He handed the paper to him.

'I think so, but I'm not sure I have all the cartridges. Especially the .44s. I'll have to check store room in back for those.'

Red wandered through the store looking at various goods on shelves, while Tyge stood outside leaning up against the building casually watching passersby. The sudden clatter of hoofs at the far end of town drew his attention. Turning he squinted up the street seeing a line of blue uniformed riders flanked by three Indians entering town. Riding up front was another man clearly not Indian or cavalry man. He wore a tall, peaked, wide-brimmed tan Stetson. Fan instantly recognized him as Nate Whitman. He looked harder a second time, pushing off the wall to be sure his eyes weren't playing tricks on him. How could Whitman be here in Whiskeytown? It seemed impossible. Yet there he was. Fan pushed through the door into Hanson's. Walking quickly up behind Cort he whispered in his ear.

'Take a look at who is riding down the street outside. And he's even got the United States Cavalry riding with him.'

Cort stepped away from the counter going to the front window. Calling Red over all three stood in disbelief as Whitman and the troopers ride by before Red spoke up.

'How in hell did he get way down here and why?'

'Horton,' said Cort. 'That's the only reason he'd be here. And it means we're clearing out soon as I get these supplies. Tyge, keep an eye on where they go while Red and I load up the horses but not out front. Bring them around to the alley in back.'

'What about our things back at camp?' Red worried.

'Leave them. There's nothing there that's important. We've got to make tracks now.'

Fan stepped back outside pulling his hat down low across his eyes watching the line of riders continue up the street past him until stopping in front of Horton's office. His hand went down to his six-gun with the same tingling anticipation he always felt when gunplay was near. If it came, he was ready for it.

'Lieutenant, your men should take a look around town while you and I see what this sheriff has to say,' Whitman ordered.

'Look for what? They don't even know what Keller looks like and neither do I.'

'I do. He rides a big, chestnut bay, with a white blaze on its chest. Another one of them has red hair and a beard to match. The others I'm not sure of, but that's a good start. Tell them to dismount so I can explain it. I'll also warn them if they do find anyone like that not to try and take them. Just get back here and we'll all go face them down together.'

'Marshal, I'll be the one giving the orders. They're my men, remember? They don't take orders from civilians, not even a lawman like you. That's my job. Please keep that in mind.'

Whitman leveled a withering stare at Stanford, someone he really didn't think was up to the job. But he needed his men and all those guns if it came to that. For once he held his tongue. 'All right, you give them the order. I'd also suggest you have them go in pairs not alone. Let's get to it, lieutenant.'

The cavalrymen separated starting down the boardwalk on each side of the street carrying their .50 caliber Sharps rifles, followed by the wondering stares of local men asking what was the United States Cavalry doing in Whiskeytown. Behind Hanson's, Cort brought out another armload of supplies while Red tied each sack on the horses, until Tyge stepped back into the store telling Cort troopers were coming up the street on foot toward the store.

'Go out back and help Red. I only have a couple of more sacks to bring out, then we can clear out of here.'

'All right, but you better make it fast. They'll be here pretty quick.'

The troopers stopped at each store front peering inside looking for anyone matching the description Stanford had given them. Reaching Hanson's they did the same, seeing a man with a sack of supplies over his shoulder heading for the back door. Turning away they continued a few steps further coming to a narrow passageway between the buildings.

'Wanna' check back there?' one said.

'We better. Stanford said not to miss anything. We'll have to squeeze through though. It looks pretty tight.'

Edging sideways one at a time the pair slowly forced their way back until they could see the alley ahead. Red and Fan were busy tying on supplies with their back to the opening when the cavalrymen stepped out into the open. Instantly they saw Red's bright red hair and beard, leveling their rifles with a shout.

'Hold it right there, you two. Put your hands up!'

Red and Fan spun in surprise, sacks still in their hands, the two uniformed men advancing on them, rifles leveled, just as Cort reached the back door hearing their warning order. He dropped the sack in his hand drawing his six-gun and rushing out on to the back porch with a shout.

'Take them, Red!'

The troopers caught by surprise, swung their rifles on Cort, giving Red and Fan that split second edge they needed to drop their goods, pulling pistols firing a sudden volley of shots matching Cort's flaming six-gun. Both cavalrymen went down writhing on the ground without getting off a single shot.

'Quick, let's get out of here!' Cort shouted leaping from the deck into the saddle, pulling his horse around wildly and spurring the big animal down the alley with Fan and Red right behind him.

'That was gunfire!' Whitman jumped from a chair in Horton's office. 'Your men must have found them.' He ran out the door with Little Hawk, Stanford and Horton behind him, all three running up the street where a small group of men was beginning to gather.

'Them shots came from that back alley!' One man pointed wide eyed, as Whitman ran up out of breath. 'I heard horses run back there too!'

Whitman tried forcing his way between buildings but could not. Instead he ran into Hanson's through the store out on to the back dock, pistol in hand, seeing both troopers dead on the ground.

'This has to be Keller and his men!' he shouted in frustration at missing the gang again.

Lieutenant Stanford stepped off the dock slowly approaching the bodies. His face was suddenly drained of color. He'd never actually seen anyone killed before, let alone his own men. Sheriff Horton came up slowly rolling both bodies over.

'These two men were . . . shot to pieces. More than one gunman did this.'

The lieutenant retreated to the dock stairs sitting with his head in both hands. 'I've got to get back to Fort Jackson, and report this disaster.' His voice was barely above a whisper.

'What you ought to be doing is getting your men together to saddle up so we can go after Keller, right now while he's still close!' the marshal countered.

'No, I've had all the advice I'm going to take from you. You cost me two good men and maybe even my officer's stripes. You want Keller, you go after him yourself. I'm done with it. My command at the fort will decide what they want to do about Keller. I only hope they don't ask me to go any further after him.'

CHAPTER EIGHT

Cort, his brother and Tyge Fan rode steadily south for the next three weeks, putting as much distance between themselves and the US Cavalry that they knew would surely come after them after killing the two troopers. They were also certain Nate Whitman must be riding with the cavalry too, but that he and the captain wouldn't know for certain exactly what direction the three would run. The trio might be outdistancing the law at least for now, but were also taking themselves deeper into equally dangerous Indian country. They were not unnoticed by a small band of Indian scouts who shadowed them day and night wondering why three white men would dare to ride into their land so foolishly. Even the United States Cavalry did not journey here without a full complement of troopers, supply wagons and their deadly 12-pound howitzer, to ward off sudden attacks.

At the southern limit of this wild and lawless country the three men reached the domain of the Jicarilla Apaches, the fiercest and most warlike of all tribes on the Colorado Plateau. The very name Apache meant 'our enemies' in the language of other Indian tribes who encountered and sometimes fought against them. After another long, difficult day riding through twisting canyon mazes thick in prickly junipers, manzanita and cliff rose, Cort pulled to a halt in a protected spot at the end of a limestone plateau. His brother was first to speak as they got down to begin unloading the horses.

'You know the farther south we ride, the farther away we get from our money still in the bank in Whiskeytown.'

'I know that,' Cort responded. 'But right now I want to get as far away from Whitman and those soldier boys as possible. We can always go back for the money. It's not going anyplace. The safest place for it is right where is in the bank.'

'I saw what I thought was riders back behind us today,' Fan spoke up. 'I only got a quick look but I don't think they were white men. Must be Indians. We'll have to be careful and keep our eyes open.'

'They've been trailing us for a while. I saw them too. As long as they stay back we'll just keep riding. We don't need any trouble from them too. We've got enough of that on our own,' Cort responded.

Red got a fire going while Tyge and Cort sorted out their supplies retrieving beef jerky and hardtack biscuits for dinner. The three men sat quietly eating, washing food down with a pull of water from their canteens. Finished eating, Tyge spoke up again.

'I don't like the idea of those Indians trailing us. Anyone else breathing down our necks only means more trouble. We don't need more of that.'

'Whether we need it or not, we've got it now.' Red looked up from the dancing flames.

'What do you mean by that?' Fan questioned.

'Because they're right here.' He nodded out to the limit of firelight, where the image of half a dozen Indians silently appeared out of the night, their rifles leveled on all three men.

They jumped to their feet ready to pull six-guns, until

Cort stopped them. 'Wait a minute. We can't shoot our way out of this. Let me try to talk to them if someone can understand me.' He slowly got to his feet, hands raised, ordering his brother and Fan to do the same.

Yellow Horse the Apache leader, stepped closer, staring first at the men then the supplies lying beyond the fire next to tethered horses. 'We are not here to fight anyone,' Cort tried a few words. 'We're just passing through. We want no trouble.'

Yellow Horse did not answer. Instead he gave a quick order. Two Apaches moved forward, untying the supply sacks and dumping everything out on the ground. Another pair yanked the three men's pistols shoving them in their waistbands. Satisfied the white men were defenseless, the Apache leader stepped up close to Cort face to face.

'Why you here?' He demanded in broken English.

'I'm glad you speak my language. Like I said, we're just passing through. We don't mean to stay here or make any trouble.'

'You with horse soldiers?'

'No. They are not our friends.'

The Apache stared harder wondering how any white man could not be friends to his own kind and especially the powerful cavalry with all their men and guns. 'You lie like all white men,' he charged.

'No, I'm not lying. The soldiers are trying to find me and my men. That's why I came far into this land. So they could not find me.'

Yellow Horse could not understand why any white man would run from the protection of soldiers. He'd never heard any white eyes ever say that before. His curiosity was aroused by such an unusual statement. He looked the three up and down noticing their worn, dirty clothes and unkempt beards. Walking around back to their horses he lifted the hoof on a big bay. The animal's shoes were worn right down to the nail heads. Back in front of Cort, he asked another question.

'Why horse soldiers look for you?'

Keller hesitated before answering this time. He wasn't sure whether to tell the truth or not. After a pause he decided to take the chance. 'Me and my men had to kill two soldiers. That's why they're trying to find us.'

The chief's inscrutable face slowly changed to surprise then begrudging admiration. 'You kill two soldiers?'

'We had to shoot our way free. We had no choice.'

Yellow Horse ordered his braves to lower their rifles. 'My people say horse soldiers come into our land. A white man with steel star rides with them. Maybe you speak truth.'

'I do. If they're riding south, they are coming after us. All we want is to stay ahead of them. If you let us leave, we'll go in the morning. We have no fight with you or your people.'

The Apache never broke his stare as Cort spoke. He looked deep into his eyes wondering if this was one white man who did speak the truth. His own braves had said the cavalry was riding south just as Cort said they would be, searching for him. He also wanted to rid his land of the cavalry any way possible. If these white men were no longer here, that could be the quickest way to avoid a major battle and the chance his village could also be raided with many old men, women and children killed. He decided on a bold plan that might solve both deadly possibilities. Explaining it with his limited English might take some doing but he was willing to try.

'I give you two braves,' He held up two fingers. 'Follow them. They show you way to Mescalero people,' he pointed into the night toward the south. 'Horse soldiers not find you there.'

Cort was stunned by the sudden offer. One minute he

thought they were going to be gunned down, the next Yellow Horse was willing to send Apache scouts, showing him the way farther south. He answered without hesitation.

'We'll follow your braves,' he nodded. 'We'll leave first thing in the morning. Our horses are worn out and tired. They need a rest. So do me and my men.'

Yellow Horse stepped back ordering his braves to give the three their guns back. He picked two of his best scouts for the ride south. Neither one spoke a single word of refusal, though the look on their dark faces said they didn't like the task before them. Going to their horses they led them in, tying them off next to Cort's.

'Ride fast,' Yellow Horse ordered. 'Go far. I want horse soldiers out of my land.'

'We will. Thank you for your help,' Cort extended his hand. The Apache did not take it or understand what it meant. Instead he turned to his men with a brief order. A moment later they disappeared back into the night followed by the sound of horses fading away.

The pair of Apache scouts spread their simple blankets on the ground well away from the three white men, sitting to quietly watch them without saying a single word.

'Not so sociable are they?' Fan stated. 'I know I won't be sleeping this night. I don't want to be knifed in the middle of the night.'

'Don't waste your time. Get some rest while you can,' Cort said. 'Those two are going to do exactly what their chief told them to. If they didn't they'd have to answer to him. I don't think any of them want to face that. I've got the feeling come sun up we're going to be doing some fast riding behind those two.'

Dawn was only a faint pink promise across the sky when Red rolled over to the prodding of a rifle barrel in his back. He jumped to his feet facing one of the scouts, wide-eyed in fear Fan's worries the previous evening had been right. Instead the dark-skinned man pointed toward his horse where the other Apache stood waiting. Red breathed a sigh of relief, leaning down and shaking his brother and Tyge awake.

'These Apaches are ready to ride. We better kick too, if we have to keep up with them. Their horses look about half wild, but they might be able to run pretty good too.'

Red's warning about following the Apaches could not have been more accurate. The pair rode fast and recklessly kicking their paint ponies down bone dry creek beds in canyon bottoms, through iron hard stands of sharp limbed manzanitas and up along narrow cliff trails barely wide enough for horse and rider next to sudden drop offs. The summer sun beat down relentlessly on men and animals until shirts were soaked dark with sweat and horses' flanks glistened in foam.

'When are those two up front going to give these animals a rest!' Red shouted to his brother riding just ahead of him.

Cort didn't answer even though he was already thinking the same thing. Fan, riding last in line, heard Red's shout, adding one of his own. 'Why don't we stop? Maybe those Indians might get the idea? They're going to run our horses into the ground like this and we'll all be afoot!'

Cort heard Tyge's shout, finally deciding he had to act. Both men were right. Kicking his laboring horse ahead faster he caught up with the second Apache in line. He signed pulling to a stop. At first the dark-skinned scout didn't understand. After a second gesture he seemed to get the idea, slowing his horse while calling to his *amigo* up front. When all four riders pulled to a stop, Cort knew his only chance to make himself understood was to try signing again. Neither Apache understood a single word of English. He extended a finger on one hand placing forked fingers on the other over the top signifying a horse and rider. Shaking his head no, he pulled the split fingers off mimicking a rider dismounting, before lifting his hand to his mouth taking an imaginary drink. For several seconds the scouts only looked at each other before one spoke a few words. The second brave slowly nodded pointing to a shady spot under tall brush where they could take a break and rest the horses. The three white men immediately took off their hats pouring water into them from half empty canteens for the horses to drink. When they were done they each had a long pull of their own to wet parched throats. Cort's signing had been a small victory, but an important one. He'd do it again in the days ahead to ask other questions he wanted the Apaches to try to answer.

If Cort and his friends thought the ride south would only last a few days or possibly even a week, they were growing more worried as that week passed into a second and the beginning of a third. Each night the Apaches still chose to spread their sleeping blankets on the ground well away from the three men. The trio never understood why, after all the days they'd spent riding together, but that was the Apache way with all white men. There was no trust especially at night. They'd been ordered to take the white men south, and that's all they were doing. No one could order them to become friends. At least the scouts knew where every hidden water hole and bubbling spring could be found. That vital knowledge alone kept men and horses alive, able to steadily keep going.

One hot afternoon the riders stopped to give the horses a rest. Cort decided once again to try to get some idea how much longer they'd be on the trail. He motioned the Apaches over, lifting both hands palms up shrugging his shoulders shaking his head before pointing ahead. The two looked at each other, puzzled at first by the odd display until one said a few words. Kneeling he picked up a small stick drawing a jagged, up and down line in flinty ground Cort took to mean mountains, kneeling next to him. The scout drew a straight line into it and a small stick figure of horse and rider before lifting three fingers pointing ahead. Keller nodded, hoping he understood. He turned to Red and Fan leaning over his shoulder.

'I think he means we'll reach mountain country in three days.'

'That's what it looks like to me too, but then what?' his brother wondered.

'I don't know. We'll have to wait and see when we get there.'

'If they cut us loose and we don't know where we are, we could still be in trouble,' Fan pointed out.

'Maybe. But at least it won't be trouble from the cavalry or Whitman. They have to be so far behind us by now that if they're still coming they'll never catch up.'

By mid-afternoon of the third day's riding, a blue line of mountains rising ahead made it clear the Apache's dust drawings had meant exactly that. Cort turned in the saddle with a small smile wrinkling his bearded face. Red nodded back while Tyge said nothing studying the high country intently. It meant cooler temperatures, more water, easier riding for them and their horses. At least it would be a break from the arid, twisted land they'd come through for so many days. Not even the Apache scouts could know they were in for a big surprise up on top.

It took half that day's riding to reach up to the pine forests and tall trees, sighing to a cool breeze. Cort looked back down across shimmering lowlands they'd struggled through now dancing in waves of heat, glad they were behind. Nearing the final ridgeline the Apaches suddenly pulled to a halt holding up their hands, staring at the figure of a lone white man sitting in the saddle, clad in buckskins watching them. Before they could react, the man called out to the scouts in their own tongue, surprising them further as he rode closer. Cort, Red and Fan also watched him approach with equal surprise. Pulling to a halt in front of the scouts the strange looking man continued talking and signing to the Apaches, glancing at the Kellers as he did so. Finishing with the scouts, he turned his attention to the trio.

'The only white men who come into this country are either on the run from the law, deserters, or lost. Neither kind lasts very long. The Mescalero Apaches kill them right quick. Which are you three?'

Cort stared back fascinated by the man's bizarre attire. He wore buckskin clothes finished off by knee high, hand made boots and leggings. Below his fur hat, long brown hair hung in a thick braid down his back, stuck with two large eagle feathers, Indian style. Around his collar he wore a pair of necklaces. One was strung with brightly colored beads. The second was a leather thong with long, white tipped claws of a grizzly bear. All in all he was some sight unlike anything the three had ever seen before or the Indian scouts either.

'If these Mescaleros are such quick killers of white men, why are you still wearing your hair?' Tyge challenged.

'Why? Because I married a chief's daughter, Blue Sky Woman. We didn't need no bible nor preacher either. We was married in the Apache way. Reckon I could say I'm part of their tribe, because of it. Names Billy Beckett. I got me a cabin down the mountain a-ways. You three would have been scalped by now if you didn't have these two braves leading you. The Mescaleros already know you're here. They sent me out to find out why. You three got a handle?'

Cort hesitated. Keller wasn't a name he wanted spread

around even way down here in the middle of nowhere. He remembered his brothers' aliases used on Loyal Horton. 'I'm John Morgan. This is Joe Brown,' he pointed to Red. He's Dade Wilson,' he nodded toward Fan. 'Are we still in Colorado Territory?'

'Ha! You mean you don't even know where you are? Boy, this is New Mexico Territory. The only thing between here and the Mexican border is Mongollon. I ride there sometimes to sell off my furs or some elk meat, and do a little trading. Once a year I might even go all the way down to Mexico. Them Mexicans pay good money for furs and hides too, like wolf, fox and big cats. Pay in gold dust or nuggets. But that's a pretty good ride from here. Takes me about two weeks, sometimes a little more. I don't like to be gone that long and leave my woman alone.'

The scouts pulled their horses around exchanging a few brief words with Beckett. Just as quickly they started away downhill without a look back.

'Those two are leaving to ride back up north to their own people. They say they've done what their chief ordered them to. Looks like you three will be on your own from here on out. That could make things mighty dangerous unless you could make your way down to Mongollon, on your own, and that ain't likely.'

Cort stared at the departing Apaches while also thinking fast. Beckett was right. On their own could be big trouble. He had a quick idea. 'How far did you say it is to this town, Mongollon?'

'From here . . . maybe a two week ride. Why you askin'?'

'Because I'm willing to pay you to take us there. You know the country and the Mescaleros, too. I don't want to have to fight my way down there even if we could find it.'

'What are you payin'?'

'How's a hundred dollars sound to you?'

Beckett didn't hesitate. 'How about two hundred? And you get to keep your hair too.'

'All right. I'll give you a hundred right now, and the other hundred when we get there.'

'You talk like you think I might take the money and run off and leave you three to the wolves?'

'No, that's just good business. You don't know us, and we don't know you. At least not yet. This way it keeps us all honest.'

'I only take hard cash or gold dust. No paper money. I don't trust that stuff.'

'I'll pay in coins, gold and silver.'

'Then we'll make medicine on it. First I want to go by my place and let my woman know I'll be gone for a while. You three come with me. We'll leave from there.'

CHAPTER NINE

Beckett's home was a long low log cabin, the back half of which went into the steep slope of the mountain side. Its thick, sod roof was supported by heavy timber beams. Three half-wild wolf dogs ran forward barking and snarling as the men rode in until Beckett shouted them back. A young Apache woman with long, black hair down to her shoulders, wearing buckskin clothes and boots, exited the cabin with a baby in her arms. Beckett eased out of the saddle, motioning for Cort, Red and Fan to do the same.

'I'll have to get some supplies before we can leave for Mongollon. You three may as well rest easy before we start. Once we do, it's gonna' be steady riding all the way. We won't stop for much except a little sleep and rest these horses. You can take your horses around back to the spring for a drink while I get loaded up.'

The buckskin-clad man held a short conversation with Blue Sky Woman, before taking the baby, lifting her over his head giving her a big, whiskery kiss. Cort looked on the unusual scene, surprised the tough-talking mountain man suddenly became a doting father. Beckett had done something else equally amazing. He'd united the Indian world, at least in this one small family with that of the white man's by taking Blue Sky Woman as his wife and having a child. It made Cort think back to his own loving childhood shared with his mother and father and brother back home in Tennessee. It seemed like a lifetime ago. Could it really have been that long, he wondered. So much had changed it was hard to believe it really had all happened. His world now was endless days running from the law and gun fights, when they closed in trying to take him. He wondered if that would ever change. Was it possible someday he could live the life of a free man, not always looking back over his shoulder for someone with a six-gun and badge, trying to take him down. At least for now that seemed only an impossible dream.

Two days ride out from Beckett's cabin the Kellers continued to discuss how far back Nate Whitman and the United States Cavalry might be. The worry never left their minds. Were they still back there somewhere trying or was it possible they'd given up finally turning back after all these days and miles. When Yellow Horse first gave them two scouts to guide them south, the long, hard days of fast riding made it seem they had to be leaving anyone trying to follow them far behind. The killing pace nearly ran their horses into the ground. With Beckett telling them they'd ridden all the way into New Mexico Territory and were now on another fast ride further south, they almost felt they could breathe easy at last. Yet that nagging question never completely went away.

For Whitman's part there was no giving up or turning back and he had plenty of company and guns to keep him going. Upon reaching Fort Jackson, with Lieutenant Stanford's tale of failure at capturing any of the Keller gang plus the death of two troopers under his command in the gunfight at Whiskeytown, he was immediately removed from leading anyone, anywhere, remanded to stay at the fort and given a menial job sitting at a desk all day shuffling papers.

In his place a new, more seasoned cavalry officer Captain Milford Darwin Longstreet took command of fifteen troopers with orders to bring the Keller gang back dead or alive no matter how long it took or how far he had to ride to accomplish it. Longstreet was a successful field-tested officer. He'd fought and won running gun battles against renegade Blackfoot Indians twice already, part of the same band that had wiped out Captain Criswell and most of his men. Both Longstreet and Whitman were a perfect match of personalities, although clashing egos would prove to be a problem sooner or later. Both lived for the notoriety of being successful, hard-nosed men who would not give up on any mission no matter how difficult it proved to be. Whitman was smart enough to know the military had the authority and legal grounds to bring the Kellers into a military court and try them there beyond his own marshal's badge. He could live with that for the final satisfaction of seeing them convicted and hung, even if it wouldn't be in his court back in Whiskeytown. He'd still share in the glory and make certain everyone knew it.

The long line of blue clad troopers with Longstreet, Whitman and Little Hawk in the lead proceeded unchallenged deeper into the land of Yellow Horse and his people. Dark eyes watched the caravan unseen with orders from their chief not to engage the white soldiers, only keeping track of their movements. If the cavalrymen somehow made a sudden turn heading for the hidden Apache village, only then would Yellow Horse order his braves to attack.

Little Hawk sensed they were being watched although both Whitman and the captain said they'd seen no sign of that. 'Apaches know we in their land,' he insisted.

'If they do, I'd like to have a little pow-wow with them,'

Longstreet suggested. 'maybe we could find out when Keller came through here and if he was still headed south like we think he is. While we're at it we might also learn where their Apache village is. After taking Keller we could come back through here and wipe out their village. This chief of theirs, Yellow Horse, could use a good hanging too. He's gotten away with bloody murder down here for far too long. I'd like nothing better than planting my regiment flag right in the middle of his village while we burn it down to the ground.'

Longstreet had a pair of trackers but not the usual Indian scouts. Instead they were white men the cavalry sometimes employed for help. Neither had ever been this far south in a land growing more difficult every day. They continually had trouble trying to stay on wind-washed hoof prints and cold, scattered fire pits left behind by the Kellers. When this happened Whitman would send Little Hawk ahead to find the way again while also trying to determine how old the sign was. By the third week of trailing it became clear the gang was still steadily heading south and might possibly continue completely out of Colorado Territory.

One evening after another long day of tough riding, Whitman sat around a smoky sagebrush campfire thinking out loud. 'I've seen this bunch run before but never so long and this far. I'm beginning to wonder if they just might go all the way into New Mexico Territory?'

Captain Longstreet stood stretching out the kinks in his back, thoughtfully sipping a cup of hot black coffee. At first he didn't reply to Whitman's remark. When he did he had some concerns of his own.

'I'll have to think about replenishing some of our supplies if we ever get near a town. So far its been nothing but sagebrush, dry creek beds and rim rock country. I had hoped by now we'd be closing in on the Kellers but that is clearly not the case. Your man Little Hawk even says the Apaches aren't following us any more. This Godforsaken country has nothing in it. I've been looking over my field maps. They say Mescalero Apache country is up ahead of us. They have a history of attacking whites both civilian and military. We could have our hands full when we reach there. Who knows? They might even find the Kellers and finish them off for us. Wouldn't that be something?'

'After as far as we've come that's about the last thing I'd want to see happen,' Whitman was quick to counter. 'That's a pleasure I've reserved for me for a long time and no one else.'

'Are you mad? It would be a perfect solution for all of us. You want the Kellers dead and so do I. If someone else does it for us, I say bravo to them. It would save us a lot more time and slow travel trying to track them down. All we'd have to do is confirm the bodies and turn back for Fort Jackson. Mission accomplished.'

'You don't understand. Finishing off the Kellers goes even beyond this badge I'm wearing. It's personal. He's made it that way. It always has been. I want to be the one who puts a bullet in all of them, but especially Cort Keller. He's mocked me personally – killing my deputy, robbing the bank in my own town not to mention taking your pay wagon and killing two of your troopers. I owe him for all of that and by God he's going to pay for it in blood as long as I live and breathe!'

The captain stared back at Whitman whose face had suddenly twisted in rage. He'd never seen him so emotionally driven. It was alarming to watch it and listen to him rant. He could not know that sheriff Mathew Buel back in Janestown had seen the very same loss of control when Whitman shot down Coy Brandon in cold blood while he tried to stop him but failed. Longstreet wondered if a man at the edge of

106

losing control over the very mention of Keller's name, had the good judgment to carry out his duties as a lawman without committing a monstrous crime of his own. At that moment the answer clearly seemed to be no.

If the captain and marshal were left wondering how far ahead the Kellers were and if they were getting any closer, both men would have been even more depressed at the good time the gang was making with Billy Beckett leading them through the mountains of New Mexico Territory. Beckett knew the way like the back of his hand and where every hidden waterhole and bubbling spring existed even on boiling hot days. He didn't have to worry about the Mescalero Apaches either, who silently watched the line of white men riding through their lands. They considered him a friend and blood brother, something the Apaches rarely did for any white man. After seven days of hard riding out from Beckett's cabin, the four men pulled to a stop, unsaddling the horses as evening shadows slowly spread misty fingers across the land. Beckett gathered wood for a small fire before opening his saddle-bags and passing around dried venison jerky and Apache acorn cakes. Red snapped off a bite of the jerky then tried the small flat pancake.

'How can I eat this? It's kind of raw, ain't it?' He held up the acorn cake.

'That's because you have to cook it before you eat it,' Billy tried not to laugh out loud but lost to chuckles, shaking his head. 'You have to rake a few coals out of the fire and put it right on top to cook for a few minutes then turn it over and cook the other side. I can tell you boys don't know much about Apaches.'

'We know how to outrun them,' Cort countered, smiling at his own small joke. 'How are we doing on time? You said it would take about two weeks to reach Mongollon. We should be half way there by now?'

'We're doing all right,' Beckett nodded looking back across the pulsing fire. 'You fellas keep up pretty good, I'd have to say that. I guess you done some riding before I took you on, huh?'

'Yeah, we've done some.' Cort wondered if Beckett was fishing for more information but didn't volunteer anything more.

'I can see you've come a-ways by the wear on your horses and gear. That goes for all of you. Really isn't any of my business, but what does bring three men way down here and not know where you're going? Most whites steer clear of this country except maybe if they got gold fever. You three don't look to me like you've got that. You've got no gear for it.'

'Let's just say we wanted to see some new country,' Red answered, as Tyge eyed Cort and Red suspiciously.

'You've seen some of that and we've still got a ways to go so you'll see a lot more of it. We're gonna come down out of these mountains into canyon country where Mongollon is. The town's in wild country hard to get to. But once talk of gold gets out men will go through hell and high water to find it. In Mongollon, the hell never left. Everyone wants to get rich. Gold fever takes over and they go wild, but you three don't look like prospectors to me. I figure you can handle all the rest of that with those fancy six-guns you got.'

'They got any law there?' Fan finally spoke up.

'Nope. No time for that yet. If the ore vein holds out they might hire themselves a star man, but not right now. Everyone's too busy digging holes like they're heading for China. It's a sight to see, that's for sure,' Beckett got to his feet turning for his bedroll. 'Let's turn in and get some sleep. We'll leave early in the morning, as usual. Good night, fellas.'

The Mongollon-bound riders were four hours out from camp the next morning when Beckett saw the dust of three horsemen behind them closing in fast. He held his hand up to halt, squinting against the sun trying to make out who it was. Still far out he identified them as Apaches by their wild riding and multi-colored horses.

'You boys just sit easy. I know these Mescaleros. What I don't know is what they're doing way down here. It must be something important to come this far to find me.'

The braves pulled sweating horses to a dusty stop, greeting Beckett in their own tongue while the Kellers looked on. The mountain man listened a moment, signing repeatedly to be certain he understood the excited talk of their unexpected guests. When finished the Apaches glanced at Beckett's three charges. The anger in their eyes was easy to read without understanding a single word they'd exchanged with the squaw man. As fast as they'd ridden in, the three braves yanked their horses around starting away. Beckett pulled at his thick beard while eyeing Cort, Red and Tyge. Before he could speak a word of the sudden encounter Cort posed a question.

'What was that all about? Your friends looked like they've run their horses pretty hard.'

'The Apaches are always hard on their animals, but those three had good reason to chase me all the way down here. Now I know why you and your friends here hired me to take you all the way to Mongolon.'

'You do, what's that?'

'They told me cavalry troopers with another white man who wears a badge, have been tracking you three. They've just come into Mescalero territory and are still far behind but coming on. They asked me if they should attack them or if I know why they're here. I told them I didn't know but so long as the soldiers didn't attack them to let them pass.

Those soldier boys must be looking for you, and to come this far doing it they must want you three pretty damn bad. What did you boys do to bring an outfit like that way down here? They've got enough guns to start another Civil War.'

Cort looked to his brother and Fan, unsure of how much to tell. Instead he did the next best thing he could think of. 'If you want to cut us lose and turn back, just tell us how far we are from Mongolon, and give us some directions. We'll try to get there on our own and you won't have to be part of anything else that might happen.'

'Wait a minute. I didn't say I wanted to cut and run for it. You paid me good money to get you there and I ain't one to welch on a deal. But I would like to know what I'm sticking my neck out for. That ain't asking too much, is it?'

'Maybe not. What I can tell you, is those soldiers and lawman the Apaches saw and us three have something personal to settle between us. We have had for a long time. I thought if we rode this far south we might avoid it at least for a while, but it looks like that won't happen now. Sooner or later we're bound to have it out face to face. The lawman has killed friends of mine and blood kin too. I owe him for that. One way or the other I'll make him pay for it. We took money from the cavalry. That's why they're riding with him. That's the whole story.'

Billy Beckett looked away for a moment thinking hard about all he'd been told. He loved living the free life, his young family, his Mescalero friends that were now kin to him. He didn't want to see any of it threatened or hurt. The sudden intrusion of the cavalry and their star man could change all that if things went wrong. He had to make up his mind and the right decision what to do right now. He turned back to the three men sitting motionless staring back. They looked tired and worn out, like he'd told them before. Hunted men all had that look. You could see it in their faces, their worn-out clothes and lean horses. Billy Beckett let out a long breath with an admission of his own.

'I can't say I've always lived on the right side of the law, either. I done some things years back I never paid up for. But I don't like it when men are hunted down like wild animals, especially when those animals are wearing badges and have twenty rifles and pistols to cut you down. No man should have to face odds like that, especially when he's got a blood feud to settle. You paid me good money to get you to Mongollon, and that's what I mean to do. What might happen after that only the Good Lord, that star man and you three will have to settle. Let's get kicking. We've still got a ways to go!'

The four men pushed their horses further south through timber clad mountains and weedy flats until slowly the land began to change. Rocky spires crumbling with age replaced tall evergreens. Steep stone canyons scoured clean of soil exposing the bowels of the earth showed spider web veins of gold and silver ore, the ageless lure that was making Mongollon the whispered word of men's dreams. Seven days later as Billy Beckett had promised, the four riders reined to a stop, looking down into a steep ravine where a shanty town interspersed with a few stone-walled buildings stood.

'It ain't much to look at, but there it is,' Beckett pointed. 'At least we can get out of these saddles and maybe get us a good hot meal before I turn back for home. The only thing between here and the Mexican border is another week's ride south through cactus and heat that would fry a horny toad.'

'Why do you bring up the border?' Cort asked.

'Because if the US Cavalry and that lawman ever get down this far, you might want to think about making the run to cross over. American law don't mean nothing down there. Once you do you're in the clear.'

The three men looked at each other, all suddenly thinking the same thing. Mexico was an idea none of them ever even considered before, not even Cort, until now that the mountain man brought it up. It might be a long shot, but what Beckett said did make sense if things ever got that bad.

'You ever crossed over?' Red questioned.

'Yeah, like I said before, when I wanted top price for my furs once in a while I'd go all the way to Cuidad Juarez. A man can get lost in Mexico and never be found. Of course I know my way around, but others might not.'

With Billy Beckett as their guide, the Kellers and Fan found the entire town of Mongollon existed on one small narrow dirt street lined with businesses of all kinds. Saloons, gambling houses, merchandise stores, a run down hotel and two restaurants graced both sides of the street while eight-horse teams of freight wagons loaded to the top board with raw ore taken from hard rock mines in the mountains around town rumbled by. Rough hewn men in dirty shirts stained dark with sweat plied the street day and night eager to spend their hard earned cash gambling, drinking and entertaining the few bar-room ladies who also made their living with men of the night.

Cort did not want to take a room in the run down Miner's Hotel. Instead Beckett helped them find an old unused cabin just uphill back of town to rent. The first night in town while all four men were eating at a small diner, shots rang out down the street as another bar fight got out of hand. Beckett eyed his three charges trying to gauge their reaction. None of them spoke up so he did.

'Gunfire around here at night is almost a regular thing. There's no law here but lots of gunpowder. You'll get used to it if you three stay here a while. If you can, just try and stay out of the way of it. I'll be heading for home and my woman tomorrow morning. I got you here like I said. All I need now is that last hundred dollars.'

'When we get back to the cabin, I'll pay up,' Cort nodded. 'You did all you promised and then some. You earned every dollar of it getting us here. The three of us will miss not having you around. We've sort of gotten used to you.'

Beckett chuckled, almost embarrassed at the compliment. 'Remember this, you three. A man can't have much of a life always having to look back over his shoulder all the time wondering if trouble is still coming. I hope you finally get some peace here, wild as this town is. Maybe it's the kind of place you can get lost in. You've come a long ways to find it.'

Next morning at the cabin the four men shook hands all around before Billy Beckett climbed into the saddle starting away with a quick wave of his hand. The three men watched him go until he was lost in sight at the far end of town. Red turned to his brother. 'I guess we're on our own now, huh?'

'One way or the other, we always have been, Red. This is just another different time and place. We ought to be getting used to it by now. I wonder if we ever will?'

CHAPTER TEN

Weeks later Billy Beckett was long gone, but his warning that the little town was a wild, lawless mining community lost deep in the Mongollon Mountains, could not have been truer. Several times each week at night the sudden roar of gunfire echoed up the street, as whiskey-eyed men who would not back down an inch settled their differences by pulling pistols and firing. The undertaker, Thurmond Heck, did a brisk business interring victims in cheap pine coffins in a weed-choked cemetery, uphill back of town. However the cost was extremely expensive because the graves had to be dynamited out of hard rock ground that pick and shovel could not penetrate. The final trip to eternity was always announced by another charge going off heard all over town.

Both Cort and his brother made it a point to spend most of their time in town during daylight hours buying food or other supplies needed at the cabin. Not Tyge Fan. He had always been a rounder, and Mongollon would be no different. Fan enjoyed noisy saloons, loud music and the company of other drinkers and gamblers. Cort continually warned him to keep a low profile, not drawing any attention to himself even though for the first time in months they seemed at last to be beyond the reach of either cavalry or a

US Marshal. Every time Cort tried to explain it, Fan refused to listen, arguing back.

'We've been on the run so long you two have forgotten how to have some fun. We're so far back in these mountains no lawman is ever going to find us. Let's live a little. I'm not going to hide each night when there's so much going on. No one here is going to bother us either. The only thing these miners know how to handle are picks and shovels. There isn't one of them who is going to stand up to us with a six-gun in their hand. They're so whiskey soaked they can't even find their way home each night. You two should come with me instead of holding up in this cabin like a couple hermits always worrying about what might happen. Let's enjoy what we have while we can.'

The Elk Horn saloon was one of Fan's favorite nighttime hangouts. The main reasons were they had a piano and fiddle player plus a beautiful, dark-eyed Mexican girl named Rita de la Vega, who sang there on weekends. Fan couldn't keep his eyes off the young woman and did not hide his growing interest. Every time she stepped up atop the bar to sing, he'd pitch five dollar gold pieces at her feet. During breaks he invited her over to his table much to complaints of other drinkers who wanted to gather around and talk to her. Tyge's quick temper and growing possessiveness finally reached the point where it became real trouble. The Elk Horn's owner, Skip Krago, came over to Fan's table one night trying to talk him into backing off.

'Listen Tyge, all these other men in here are paying customers too. If you don't let them mix with Rita, it's going to lead to trouble. I don't need that. I'm asking you man to man to back off a little bit. I don't want to have to tell you you can't come in here any more.'

Fan stared back hard, his light blue eyes seemingly looking right through Krago, as if he wasn't even there.

115

'You'd be making a real big mistake, trying something like that,' he finally said. 'If you know what's good for you, you'll forget about that.'

Krago instinctively leaned back at the obvious threat but would not back down. 'Remember what I said,' he got to his feet looking down on Fan. 'Rita works here for everyone to enjoy. Not just you. I don't want to have to tell you again.'

Nearing his home Billy Beckett finally topped a long ridge leading down to his cabin. It had been a long, grueling ride getting back home from Mongollon. He gave his tired horse a rest, his eyes wandering over twisted lowlands far below, the same country he'd first seen the Kellers and their Indian scouts come through so many weeks ago. It took a moment before he leaned forward studying something. Were his eyes playing tricks on him? He squinted harder shading them with both hands. He could barely make out a long, thin line of riders moving closer. Instantly he knew it had to be the cavalry and the US Marshal Cort had told him about. They were still trailing the three men he'd befriended. For just a fleeting moment he considered turning around and riding back to Mongollon warning them. Yet, his home, Blue Sky Woman, and baby daughter were only another half hour's ride down the ridge. He struggled with his conscience and mixed emotions. He'd left his family alone long enough. He didn't want to do that again, and especially not now with these military people and lawman riding into his land. He sat in the saddle watching the distant images coming closer.

'Damnit,' he muttered under his breath. 'I just hope those boys keep their eyes open like I told them to. I can't be in two places at the same time, much as I'd like to.' Beckett pulled his horse around starting down the ridge without looking back, praying he'd made the right decision.

Little Hawk riding in the lead reined his horse to a stop, his eyes studying the long climb up the mountains ahead of him. His sharp eyes scoured the ground closer as Whitman and Longstreet rode up alongside him.

'What do you think?' Whitman asked. 'Are we still on their trail?'

The young Crow nodded, never taking his eyes off pine topped ridges along the skyline. 'They come through here.' He pointed to a dim trail winding up the first hills.

'Any idea how long ago?' The marshal questioned.

'Long time. Hoof prints almost gone.'

Captain Longstreet eyed both Whitman and his sidekick before looked up into the high country ahead. Tracks so old they were hardly visible, was the last thing he wanted to hear. For the first time since the long chase began weeks ago, he started wondering if they would ever catch up to the Kellers. Instead of closing in on them it seemed they were only chasing ghosts. Supplies for his men were running so low he'd put them on half rations. Visions he once harbored of grandly riding back into Fort Jackson, with the gang in handcuffs, were fading as fast as their tracks. He'd relied heavily on Whitman's boast he knew the Kellers' every move personally, and they would soon run them down. That was clearly not the case either. The tired officer took a long pull on his canteen thinking all this over. Maybe, he concluded, the time had come to set a deadline on how far he was still willing to extend the chase before turning back. He knew the marshal would balk at the suggestion, but he didn't have to answer to superior officers and orders. He did, and his career depended on results of those orders.

'Before we go any further, I think the time has come for us to have a frank discussion,' he addressed Whitman who was still questioning Little Hawk.

117

'About what?' The marshal turned in the saddle.

'I'm short on rations. It doesn't appear to me we're getting any closer to these men and now we've got a long climb up into these mountains to who knows where or what? From what you told me when we started I expected us to have them dead or in irons by this time. Instead we're getting nowhere. Much more of this and I'll have to turn back for the fort, like it or not.'

'You'd quit me cold just like that?' Whitman's face turned red with anger. 'Do you realize what you're doing if you cut and run? You'd be the laughing stock of the entire fort!'

'I cannot push my men until they've got no fight left in them. That would be a total dereliction of duty. I don't expect you to understand this. You're not a military man.'

'I don't have to be a military man to know a quitter when I see one. You want that on your record?'

'There are limits on what any man can take except maybe for these Kellers. They've managed to stay far ahead of us and never seem to change pace or stop to rest. Your own man even said so himself. The tracks we've been following are so old he can barely stay on them.'

'But he has stayed on them and he just told me when we get up into these mountains it will be easier to follow them. You can't turn back now. This is the break we've been waiting for. I've got a sworn duty to bring these murderers back to face justice and likely in your own court. By God I mean to do exactly that. Give it at least one more week. Don't turn back on me now. You'll regret it if you do, and so will your career.'

Longstreet stared back. Another five or six days of this would be all he and his men could take. He wiped sweat off his face with a bandanna considering all that had been said. 'All right, but that's it. We don't get any closer than we have been, you're on your own and that's final!'

Three hours riding brought the caravan to the last high ridge along the skyline.

Captain Longstreet ordered his men to dismount giving the horses a blow, while Little Hawk eased out of the saddle walking several yards studying the ground leading down the ridge. He motioned Whitman over for a brief conversation.

'Four riders go down there,' he pointed. 'Come back same way.'

'Four, are you certain?'

He nodded. 'They go that way.' He pointed off to the south.

'Little Hawk is on them again,' Whitman shouted to the captain. 'I told you he'd pick them up, didn't I? They're heading south like they've been doing from the start. Let's keep moving on them. By now they don't think anyone is still following them, but we are and we'll catch up to them if you don't turn rabbit on me and run for it.'

The officer walked over irritated at the slur and Whitman's boast, but with a question of his own. 'Your man says these tracks go down this ridge then come right back up again?'

'Yes, that's what Little Hawk says, why?'

'That's my question, why would they do that? What's down there they'd take the time to ride to? If it's as good a track as he says it is, I say we should at least take the time to follow them and see what's so important before we go running off in the other direction.'

'I say that's a waste of good time,' Whitman shot back. 'we know all of them left still riding south. That's the way we need to keep going, not stop for some side trip they might have made!'

'These are my men and I'll use them as I see fit. I'm not going to leave any stone unturned at this late date.

119

I'm following them down.'

'We don't have time for it. We need to keep moving while we still have daylight left, not go off on some wild goose chase!'

'I'm going to take half my men and follow them. I'll leave the other half with you, if you insist on running off. Leave markers for us to follow. We'll catch up to you when I've satisfied my suspicions. If we don't catch up before dark, build a good fire so we can find you.'

'Build a big fire? Every Apache in these mountains will see that!'

'There's no other choice. Of course you can always wait right here until we come back up and all leave together like we should.'

The marshal's jaw tightened in anger. He glanced at Little Hawk, shaking his head. It was senseless bandying words with Longstreet and his straightjacket military thinking. 'I won't sit here and wait for you when you could be gone for hours, can't you see that? How much more obvious does it have to be, to get that through your head!'

'Remember to mark the trail and build a fire if you have to. I'm following these tracks. I'll come back up when I get my answer.'

The captain walked back to his men picking out six troopers plus his two civilian trackers. The remainder he ordered to go with Whitman.

One of his trackers, Gus Teague, walked over studying the faded hoof prints Little Hawk had pointed out.

'Can you stay on them?' Longstreet questioned under his breath.

'I'm pretty sure I can. Especially here in this soft ground.'

'Mount up!' the captain ordered, his troops stepping up into their saddles. 'Teague, you take the lead. Have Ryder stay up front with you too for help if you need it. Move as fast as you can. I don't want the marshal to get ten miles away if I can help it. I'd never hear the end of his moaning about it.'

Billy Beckett had split enough wood for the evening fire. He was halfway back to the front door with an armload, when he heard the sound of many horses coming closer down through timber. He knew it wasn't the Apaches. Their shoeless horses didn't make that kind of heavy thudding. He also knew that could only mean trouble of some kind. It had to be that column of cavalrymen he'd seen earlier from high up on the ridge. He dumped the wood on the ground as the first blue clad horsemen broke out of timber. Stepping quickly into the cabin he warned Blue Sky Woman not to come outside. She started to ask why before he stopped her with a finger to his lips, quickly closing the door and turning to face the riders pulling to a stop. Longstreet eased out of the saddle, eyeing the cabin, corral out back and animal hides stretched on wooden frames. Snarling, wolf dogs ran up before Beckett shouted them back.

'Hello,' the captain boldly walked up extending a hand Beckett did not take. Unperturbed he continued. 'My name is Captain Milford Darwin Longstreet, United States Cavalry, nearly a month out of Fort Jackson. You've got quite a place here. Obviously you've lived here a long time.'

'Why would a man need three names?' Beckett mocked the officer. 'Two does pretty well for most men.'

'And yours is?'

'I'm called Beckett by any white man who needs to know. The Apaches called me something else you wouldn't understand.'

Longstreet ignored the second insult. He'd already

begun to realize the buckskin clad man with feathers in his long, dark hair would not help him, but he forged on. 'We picked up your tracks on the ridge. You were riding with three other men. I'd like to know who they were?'

Beckett didn't answer for several seconds, still eyeing the officer with contempt. He knew whatever he said could mean big trouble for the friends in far away Mogollon. He had to be double careful not to give anything away.

'They were trapper friends of mine,' he finally ad-libbed.

'Trappers? We've been following those same tracks for weeks, and they weren't made by any trappers. The men who made them are named Keller. They're wanted by the United States government for robbery and murder of federal troopers. Anyone who hides them or knows where they are, refusing to answer, can also be taken into custody. Do you expect me to believe some cock and bull story about trappers?'

'Believe what you want. I didn't invite you down here, so you'll have to find your own way back up. I've said all I'm going to say. I've got chores to do. The sooner you ride out, the sooner I can get to them.'

The muffled sound of a baby crying inside the cabin only lasted long enough for Longstreet to hear it before Blue Sky Woman silenced the little girl. It was exactly the edge he needed to make his threat stick. 'So, you have a woman in there and a child too. You want to be taken in irons back to Fort Jackson, and leave them here to fend for themselves?'

Beckett didn't flinch at the threat. Instead his temper boiled up. 'First of all you'd have to come back here and find me. Second, even if you could I'd have you riding around in circles following your own tracks. Third, if you ever did catch up I'd have the whole Apache nation come down on you. There ain't enough of you soldier boys in Fort Jackson to get out of that alive. Now I'm done jawing with you. Saddle up and ride out of here before I really lose my temper!'

'I'll be back, Mr. Beckett. You can count on it. I won't forget you and your lawless attitude either.'

'Remember what I said. You come back here and threaten my woman and child, you better bring the whole US Army with you, because you're gonna' need it!'

Longstreet saddled up as his men stared in disbelief at the vicious encounter. None of them had ever heard an officer challenged so boldly either from another cavalry officer and certainly not a civilian dressed like an Indian. Several troopers glanced around uneasily wondering if the Apaches Beckett had threatened were watching and waiting for word from the Squaw Man to attack. Once they started up the trail heading for the top, they still constantly twisted in the saddle looking behind them, fearing an ambush.

Marshal Whitman had pushed Little Hawk and the rest of the men with him as fast as he dared on the tracks. Occasionally when they were lost, the Crow scout would double back picking them up again going forward. Whitman wanted to leave the captain as far behind as possible, forcing him to struggle to catch up and pay for his stubborn insistence to follow the trail downhill to Beckett's cabin. Mountain night comes down fast like a lantern suddenly being snuffed out. The first bright rise of a July Buck Moon helped the riders keep going another hour longer before Whitman finally pulled to a stop in a copse of evergreens.

'You men gather up some firewood so your precious captain can try to find us. I wouldn't be a bit surprised if it takes him until sun up tomorrow morning. It would serve him right to wander around half the night.'

'Should we make it big, like he said?' a private asked.

'No. Make one we can keep warm with. I don't want a bonfire inviting every Apache in these mountains to come riding in on us. If Longstreet can't see it, that's his problem not mine. I'll post two of you for night watch so the rest of us can get some sleep. Be sure to picket our horses on a rope line. I don't want them wandering off either. I want to get an early start in the morning, whether he shows up or not.'

Far behind, Captain Longstreet continually berated his two trackers for not moving fast enough and losing the trail several times as light faded and long shadows of evening reached out, beginning to cover the land in darkness forcing the riders to pull to a halt.

'Teague, you and Ryder go out a ways farther and see if Whitman has a fire going someplace ahead. If he does, we'll keep on going until we catch up. If not, we'll have to make a quick camp here until dawn.'

Teague looked back at the officer in amazement. 'Neither me or Ryder can see in the dark, Captain. It makes no sense for us to do that now. Besides we're well into Apache country by now and if they're out there close by, we'd just be riding into an ambush. I'm not looking to invite myself to a scalping.'

'I gave you an order. Can you understand that? If you want to get paid when we get back to Fort Jackson, I expect you to carry it out and not moan about Indians and scalpings. Ride out there and look for that signal fire. I won't tell you again!'

Teague turned away in disgust, motioning Ryder to follow him heading for their horses. Once out of earshot of Longstreet, he gave his own orders. 'We'll ride out just far enough they can't hear the horses, then wait a while before coming back. And that's as far as we're going. I'm not about to go wandering around in the dark like some damn fool asking to end up staked over a mound of red ants. Come on!'

CHAPTER ELEVEN

The same Buck Moon that helped Nate Whitman keep riding after dark, was fading out at dawn when Tyge Fan stepped out of the Elk Horn saloon, with his arm wrapped tightly around Rita de la Vega's waist. Fan had ignored Skip Krago's warning not to monopolize the beautiful young woman's time. The more he sat each night watching her sing while smiling seductively and circulating among paying customers, the more he wanted her only to himself and no one else. Rita knew it too and used it to stoke his jealousy. She loved the attention. Tyge wasn't sure if his affections were love or lust, and he didn't care. He'd never met or seen another woman like her, and his fascination only grew. Her dark flashing eyes, long black hair and full lips, hypnotized him completely. He sat for hours watching her perform.

Skip Krago had warned Fan several more times after the original incident not to keep trying to take up all Rita's time while she was working. Tyge continued to ignore the warning. He was younger than Krago. His swaggering walk and bold talk made it clear he'd be faster on the draw with that fancy six-gun hung low on his hip, if it ever came to that. Krago finally felt it was time to teach Tyge a lesson he wouldn't forget, but not by dirtying his own hands to carry it out. Instead he'd buy the muscle he needed. Plenty was available.

Mongollon was a town full of loud, tough, grimy men who made their back-breaking living swinging picks, shovels and lighting off dynamite charges deep down in dark, dangerous mine tunnels blasted through hard rock mountains. After a day's sweat and labor they spent nights in town raising whiskey hell, spending all their money, broke before next pay day. Anyone offering a shiny twenty dollar Liberty gold piece, could buy their services from a simple back alley beating to ambush murder for an additional twenty. Krago's office safe in the back room of the Elk Horn was stacked with three heavy steel trays of Liberty twenties. He picked out two of his toughest customers, hiring the pair with a promise of an additional twenty each to teach Fan a lesson he'd never forget. He didn't want a killing. That was too messy, too many questions asked even in this wild town with no law. Just a good, bloody beating would deliver the message he wanted. The two men were all too eager to make a fast forty dollars, waiting in an alley next to the Elk Horn, when Fan and Rita stepped out that morning.

As the love birds passed, both men stepped out, each carrying a hardwood axe handle. One grabbed Rita from behind yanking her backwards to the ground as she screamed with fear. His partner viciously swung his club hard across Tyge's back legs collapsing him with a sudden shout of excruciating pain. 'This is a message from Mr Krago!' the second alley man shouted, stepping over the top of Fan, lifting the club high over his head with both hands for another crippling blow. Fan twisted on the ground yanking his six-gun out of its holster and firing one thundering shot straight up. The bullet caught the big man under his whiskered chin collapsing him in a heap, dead atop Fan who struggled trying to roll him off. His partner ran forward swinging his club until Rita got to her feet leaping on to his back clawing his face with long, sharp fingernails on both hands. He screamed in pain, twisting and trying to throw her off, giving Fan precious seconds to stagger upright on shaky feet. His six-gun roared again, the bullet impact driving the miner backwards. Rita fell off screaming at the man in Mexican, as he rolled on the ground moaning loudly, grabbing his stomach. She ran to Tyge's side helping him stand on battered legs. Suddenly emotion swept over her and she began to cry, wrapping her arms around him while he still gripped the pistol tight in his hand.

The few men still on the street ran up eyeing the wild scene all asking questions at the same time. 'What just happened here!' one man asked, looking down on the two bodies.

'Hey,' another man cut him off. 'That's Frank Brice and Leon Coons. They work up at the Deep Six Mine, or they did until now.'

'They tried to bushwack me and my woman,' Tyge answered. 'They would have if I didn't stop them.'

'Why would anyone want to do that?' the first man questioned.

Skip Krago suddenly ran out the front door of the Elk Horn, looking up the street, wild eyes at the sudden carnage. He stopped dead in his tracks staring at Fan, Rita and the other men standing over the bodies. Very slowly he began to retreat step by step back toward the door, still facing them with his hands lifted palms up. 'I'm not armed. Don't do something you'll be sorry for, Fan. You'll hang if you do!' His voice broke in fear as he shouted.

'You're the one who'll hang, Krago. And I'll be right here to help them tie the knot around your skinny neck, if I don't kill you first!' Tyge shouted back starting the six-gun toward the saloon owner until Rita grabbed his arm pulling it away.

'No, Tyge, please don't do it. I don't want to be part of any more killing!' More tears began running down her face until she wrapped both arms around Fan who fought back the urge to pull the trigger. Instead, he slowly holstered the wheel gun, trying to comfort her, but he wasn't done yet.

'You're going to have to face me one way or the other, before I leave this town,' he warned Krago. 'I know you're behind this. I'll make you pay for it. It's just a matter of time. Remember what I said!'

Krago disappeared inside the saloon, Tyge continuing to lean on Rita for support. It was obvious the crushing blows had nearly crippled him. The small group of men surrounding the pair saw it too.

'We ain't got no doctor here,' one said. 'you'd best get off your feet with those shaky legs of yours.'

Fan nodded, looking Rita in the eyes. 'Help me get up to my cabin,' his breath came in short gasps as the pain soared. 'I can rest there. Let's get to it while I can still stand up.'

The moderate climb to the cabin took every ounce of strength Tyge could muster. Before he reached the front door, both Cort and Red came outside watching him and Rita slowly coming closer. It was clear something was wrong with Fan the way he struggled step by slow step, stopping frequently to steady himself.

'We heard shots,' Cort called out. 'I hope it didn't have anything to do with you two?'

Tyge didn't answer, finally making it to the front door. The brothers eyed him as he leaned on Rita, his face twisted with pain. Without his answer, both Kellers knew he was involved. Once inside Fan lowered himself groaning on to a bunk with Rita helping him. After slowly stretching his legs out, he admitted what the shooting was all about. Cort and Red exchanged quick glances when he was finished.

'That's the worst thing you could have told me,' Cort shook his head turning away, trying to hold his temper. 'I told you not to start any trouble. Instead you've gone and done exactly that so everyone in town will begin to wonder about all three of us, not only you. We might have to pack up and run again, just when we found someplace to stop and take it easy for a while. And all because of this woman, which I also told you would be trouble. Why don't you listen to me when I warn you about things like this? You want all of us to get hung by a gang of vigilantes?'

Tyge might be in real misery, but he instantly met Cort's anger with his own. 'I had no choice. Did you hear what I just said? Those two bums would have beat me, and Rita, to death, if I didn't stop them. And don't try to lecture me on who I can see and who I can't. There's nothing perfect about you either. Why do you think we've been on the run for over a month? It's because of your doings between you and Whitman. Take a look at yourself, Cort, before you start yelling at me. You ain't my daddy!'

Fan struggled pulling himself upright on the bunk. His eyes narrowed to angry slits, as his hand moved down toward his six-gun. Rita quickly grabbed his arm.

'Don't do that, Tyge. Please don't,' she begged, wrapping her arms around him trying to force him back down. 'I don't want anymore trouble.'

'That does it,' Fan shouted, trying to push her off. 'I'll get my gear and get out of here. You two see how far you get on your own without me backing you up. I want my share of the money too, and I want it right now!'

'All right. You called it. Maybe it's best we do split up. I'll get your money. Your horse is out back, if you can even get on him.' Cort turned away.

'But Tyge, where will you go?' Rita cupped his face in her hands, fearful she would lose him if he was forced to leave town.

'Don't worry. I'm not going far. I'm moving in with you and your mother and father.' He stunned her wide eyed with his sudden demand. 'I'll pay them to put me up. They'll need the money, because you're not working at the Elk Horn anymore either. I'll be the only cash they have, now!'

Rita groped for words that would not come, slowly shaking her head until she was finally able to take a deep breath regaining the power to speak. 'But . . . you cannot do that, Tyge. My mother and father will not allow it. You have to understand why . . . please try.'

'Who is going to stop me, Rita? Are you, or either of them? You just tell them that's the way it's going to be and don't worry about anything else. They were living off the money you made working for Krago. That's gone now, but I've got plenty of cash. Help me up so I can get my gear. We're leaving here!'

After paying Fan his cut of the money, Cort and his brother stood at the door watching Tyge slowly hobble down slope toward town, while Rita led his horse.

'Looks like we're down to two,' Red put a hand on his brother's shoulder.

'That's the way we started out, remember?' Cort turned toward him with a grim smile on his lips. 'Maybe it's the way it has to be.'

'Yeah, I do remember. It seems a long, long time ago, brother.'

'Almost half a lifetime,' Cort replied. 'I wonder what the other half will bring?'

Fan forced his way into the small de la Vega adobe at the far end of town. Rita's mother and father spoke very little

131

English, only enough to get by on. Both were terrified of Fan's sudden presence, avoiding him as much as possible even in the same house. Rita tried in vain to explain away the tense situation, but as far as the elderly couple were concerned their daughter had suddenly chosen a life of sin they were helpless to understand or change. Bewildered, they rarely talked to her either.

Tyge's legs slowly heeled over the following weeks but he still walked with an obvious limp that would never completely vanish. When he and Rita walked down the narrow street of Mongollon, other men passed with furtive glances without a word of greeting. His quick temper reputation and gun speed preceded the pair everyplace they went. Tyge Fan was someone to avoid at all costs. Even his old friends the Keller brothers went out of their way not to run into him. Another man stood at the grimy, front window of the Elk Horn saloon watching Fan and Rita pass arm in arm. Skip Krago stared longingly at the beautiful Mexican girl who'd once sung in his establishment, remembering his own personal plans to get close to her. That was before Fan began dominating her time and causing trouble. He'd not only taken Rita away from him, but even killed the two men he'd hired to beat fear into him. Krago would not forget what Fan had done but would not directly try to confront him again. That was too dangerous, as everyone in town already knew. But if he ever had the chance to get even in some other way, he'd strike fast as the deadly diamondback rattlesnakes that infested the mountains around town.

After another Saturday night of Tyge and Rita making the rounds drinking and dancing late in several other saloons, Sunday morning found Fan lying in bed with a whiskey hangover, while Rita got up and dressed. She leaned down running a slender hand through his tousled hair. 'Tyge, I have to go to town and buy some flour and salt for tortillas. I need some money to do so, hon.'

Tyge rolled over his head pounding, irritated she'd disturbed him. 'Wait . . . we'll go later . . . when I get up,' he ordered sleepily burying his head under the covers.

'But I have to go now. We have nothing to eat. Please give me some money and I'll go while you sleep.'

Fan uttered an insult under his breath before groping for a leather pouch on the small table next to the bed. Extracting a fistful of silver coins, he tossed them on the end of the bed, rolling back over without another word. Rita quietly scooped up the money leaving the room.

'You're up early, Miss de la Vega,' Thomas Fulton, owner of Fulton's Dry Goods store greeted Rita as she came through the front door.

'What can I get for you this fine morning?'

She flashed a half-hearted smile, ordering a sack of flour, tin of lard and salt. While Fulton headed for the back room to retrieve the flour, Rita's attention was suddenly drawn to the street outside where the sound of many horses passing by drew her attention. She went to the front window looking out seeing a line of dusty uniformed cavalrymen as they passed, before pulling to a stop in front of the Elk Horn. Fulton came back to the counter, quickly putting the flour down and joining her at the window.

'I thought I heard horses. I haven't seen a military outfit like that in years,' he commented, adjusting his spectacles.

'Why would they be here?' Rita wondered out loud.

'I don't know. Maybe the Apaches are on the warpath again. That's about the only thing I can think of why they would be way down here. Usually they stay up north near Fort Jackson. Looks like they even have a US Marshal with them. See that man just getting down? I saw he had a badge on.'

The phrase 'marshal' suddenly made Rita's heart beat faster. Tyge never revealed much about his earlier life before riding into Mongollon, however she'd remembered he'd once said something about wanting to kill a US Marshal. Could this star man riding with the cavalry be that kind of man. She did know Fan had lived outside the law, even though he never explained any events or details.

'I've got to get home,' she said turning away from the window. 'What do I owe you?'

Rita ran as fast as she could all the way back to the adobe house on the hill, arriving out of breath. Hurrying into the bedroom, she found Fan still sound asleep. 'Tyge, wake up, honey. I have to tell you something important.'

Fan opened one eye glaring at her. 'Why do you keep doing this? Can't you see I'm trying to sleep off last night? Wake me when my breakfast is ready.'

'No, you have to listen to me. A bunch of soldiers and a marshal just rode into town. I remember you once said something about a marshal. I ran all the way to. . . .'

Fan suddenly threw off the covers leaping to unsteady feet struggling to pull on pants, a shirt and his boots. Strapping on his six-gun, he grabbed Rita hard by her shoulders.

'I've got to go. Get my horse out back and grab my saddle too. I'll be out there soon as I pack up a few things. Move!'

'Go, go where, why?' Her face instantly twisted in fear.

'Don't ask me any questions now. I don't have time to explain it. Just do what I say, and hurry up!'

In their cabin on the far side of town, Cort and Red had also seen the troopers riding downhill into town. They were busy doing exactly the same thing, packing fast. 'I don't know how Whitman followed us all the way down here, but we don't have time to worry about it,' Cort said, shucking into his jacket.

'Yeah, I thought at last we'd found someplace to take it easy for a while,' Red answered. 'What about Fan, should we warn him too?'

'Tyge decided to cut us loose, remember? Not the other way around. He's on his own. We've got to get the horses saddled and get out of here fast.'

'Where we going?'

'The only place left is Mexico.'

'Mexico? We don't even know how to get there.'

'Yes we do. Remember what Beckett said? It's due south about a week's hard ride away. That's where we're headed, brother. And once we get there maybe we can stop running once and for all.'

'Why is that?'

'Because US law doesn't mean anything once we cross the border. We'll be in the clear. Let's get to it!'

Captain Longstreet, Nate Whitman and Little Hawk stepped down out of the saddle in front of the Elk Horn, as a growing crowd of passersby formed a curious circle around them. Before Longstreet could utter a word, Whitman took over as usual.

'Men, we've been on the trail of three killers we think might be here in town. We've ridden a long ways getting here and don't want to miss them now. Their names are Tyge Fan, and the Keller brothers, Cort and Red. If any of you know even one of these men I want you to speak up and tell us about it right now.'

'You came to the right place,' Krago immediately stepped forward. 'This man Fan, lives in a house at the far end of town. He's already caused enough trouble around here even killing two of my own men. He was around town just last night. I'm pretty certain he still is.'

'Can you take me to this house you're talking about?' Whitman asked.

'You bet I can.'

'Take one of our trooper's horses and let's get up there. I don't want him or the other two to slip away again!' the marshal ordered.

Tyge hurriedly stuffed personal belongings in two cloth sacks. His money and extra cartridges were next before he could buckle up both saddle-bags. Tossing the sacks over his shoulder he grabbed the heavy leather bags with his other hand yelling out for Rita, at the top of his lungs.

'You got my horse ready?'

There was no answer. He ran through the house toward the back door calling her again. "Rita, do you hear me. I've got to get going!'

Kicking open the door he came to a sudden stop. A line of cavalry men stood in front of their horses forty feet away, rifles leveled on him while Little Hawk held one arm around Rita's waist and the other one over her mouth as she struggled trying to break free to warn him.

'Think you're going someplace, Fan?' Whitman relished asking the question taking a few steps forward. 'Tell me where your pals are and I won't even kill you where you stand. Instead I'll take you back to Fort Jackson, to hang.'

'You go straight to hell,' Tyge yelled back. 'No matter what happens to me, I'll take you down before I go!'

'You think so? There's a dozen rifles aimed at you. Before you can draw a breath they'll cut you down like ripe wheat. I'll drop the hammer on you too. I won't ask you again. Where are the Keller brothers? Spit it out and you'll live a little longer!'

Tyge let the saddle-bags fall from his hand shrugging the

136

sacks off his shoulder. He squared off against Whitman and the line of troopers, his right hand dropping to his six-gun. 'Let's see just how fast you are, Whitman!'

Cort and Red kicked their horses up canyon, topping out on the rim, pulling to a quick halt looking back toward Mongollon. The sudden sound of thundering rifle shots echoed across the valley mixed with the single crack of a six-gun. Red turned to his brother.

'They found Fan,' was all he said.

'Maybe, but they won't find us. Let's kick for the border!'

A wisp of dust twisted up into the air as the brothers spurred their horses away disappearing into a thick tangle of cedars heading south. Mexico and safety beckoned, if they could make it to the border first.

CHAPTER TWELVE

After Tyge Fan's body was removed from the de la Vega home, Captain Longstreet, Marshal Whitman and Little Hawk searched the abandoned cabin Cort and Red had stayed in. They'd left Rita hysterical with grief collapsed in her mother's arms. Skip Krago, ever the 'good citizen', had directed them to this location too. Once the trio was satisfied the Kellers had indeed lived there, they stepped back outside discussing their situation. It clearly became a serious predicament for at least one of them.

'I had hoped we'd finish off all three of these men right here in Mongollon,' the captain took off his hat wiping sweat from his brow. 'Instead, we only got Fan. There's no telling where the other two on the run went now. I'm going to have to seriously consider ending, at least for now, my part in going any further. My men have been pushed to their limit and so have I. Sooner or later these Kellers will show up someplace else again. Where, only God knows. If and when they do, myself or some other cavalry officer will go after them again. Their kind never changes. They'll rob and kill drawing attention to themselves. There is no doubt in my mind they'll both end up hanging because of it. I've done all I can. It's time for me to turn back.'

'Have you lost all your backbone?' Whitman walked up

face to face challenging the officer. 'You can't quit now and run like a jackrabbit for the fort. We've already killed Fan, and nearly got the Kellers too. We've run them all the way down here and now is the time to finish the job, not turn tail and give up. There's no place left for them to go. You abandon me now and you'll never live it down!'

'I told you weeks ago if we didn't catch up to them soon, I'd have to turn back. There's no one "abandoning" anyone. I stayed on because you said your man could track them down. He did, but we only got one of them. From what Mr Krago told me, the only thing south of here is the Mexican border, if that's the way they went. He says it's another hard week's ride away. I've stretched my men and supplies to the limit. Can't you understand that?'

'Will you listen to reason? The Kellers are no more than a few hours ahead of us. We've never been this close to them before. We might be able to run them down if we stop standing here arguing about it and ride out after them right now. What's another four or five days after the weeks we've spent getting this far!'

Longstreet turned away from the marshal nearly shouting in his face. He was tired of Whitman's constant badgering and liked it even less in front of his men. It was equally bad for their moral, if they had any left. He walked to his horse retrieving a canteen and taking a long slow drink as he struggled about what to do next. What if the marshal was right and they could finally run the Kellers down. The thought that worried him most was he'd be back at Fort Jackson, admitting defeat, while Whitman and his sidekick possibly rode down the brothers, bringing them back in handcuffs. It would look like he'd given up when success was within his grasp. That would be a black mark on his military record too risky to chance. The marshal stood a few yards away, hands on his hips, waiting for an answer.

The captain pushed the cork back in the canteen top, taking a deep breath before turning around. He tightened his belt straightening his shoulders.

'I'll take my men as far as the border, and that's absolutely the end of it. If we don't close in on the brothers by then, I'm done with it!'

'All right, let's get to it. We've already wasted enough time standing here.' Whitman turned for his horse with Little Hawk right on his heels.

Cort and his brother could not help but notice the land changing as they pushed themselves and their worn-out horses farther south each day under the relentless hammer of a blistering sun. Rough stone cliffs and mountains tinged in tall pines surrounding Mongollon gave way to lower, treeless hills and brushy flats devoid of even a drop of water. Sweat soaked and bone tired, the pair kept riding each day speaking little, hats pulled low against the blinding glare, squinting ahead for some small piece of shade to stop and rest in. At night they built no fire, too tired to try, always fearful if they were still being followed someone behind might see the distant blink of flickering light. Rolling up in their one wool blanket, the cruel heat of day suddenly turned into chilling night as they struggled through fitful sleep. Day after day they drove themselves up again, always on the move, always angling south, for another twelve hours of mind-numbing heat.

In misty shadows before another dawn, Cort woke sitting up wrapping the thin blanket around his shoulders, trying to count how many days he and Red had been struggling to reach the border. Was this seven or eight? He'd lost count and couldn't remember. Hungry, tired, trying to gird himself for another day's ride, he looked off to the south as the sky brightened. For a moment he thought his eyes were playing tricks on him. He rubbed them before trying to focus again. It looked like the tiniest halo of light that was not dawn. He slowly got to his feet studying the strange apparition. It had to be some kind of light still hidden beyond undulating hills ahead. He shook Red awake.

'What . . . is it?' Red sleepily lifted himself up on one elbow. 'Time to go?'

'Look out there up ahead. I think I see some kind of light, but I don't know what?'

Red grunted, getting to his feet, following Cort's out-stretched arm. 'Ahh . . . it can't be any fire. There's nothing in this desert to burn except rocks and mesquite.'

'Let's saddle up and head for it.' Cort turned for the horses.

The brothers rode ahead until the undulating land eventually opened up to a long downhill slope with an expansive view across miles of desert flats stretching far away to a distant line of mountains low along the skyline. Halfway between mountains and riders they could just make out a cluster of low, flat-topped buildings still many miles away, the first sign of civilization they'd seen in nearly two weeks. Tiny pinpoints of flickering light from coal oil lamps was the source of the glow Cort had seen.

'We've made it to someplace,' Red said.

'Yes, but where? Are we still in America or Mexico?'

'There's only one way to find out. We can finally get these horses and ourselves a good feed and watering. My belt buckle is pulled up so far I had to cut a new notch in it to keep my pants up.'

Riding closer to the modest size community the first thing the Kellers noticed was almost all buildings were made of either adobe or a few of stone. Entering the first dirt street they started down a row of dark store fronts still closed. All signs painted on their front walls were written in

141

Mexican. Cort reined to a stop turning to his brother.

'From the looks of this, I'd say we'd finally made it into Mexico. If I'm right, we're home free, brother!'

Red leaned forward on the saddle horn, rubbing his tired face with both hands, turning to look down the empty street. 'I just hope you're right, because neither me or this horse of mine could have made it another day out there.' He pulled a thumb over his shoulder, at the desert growing in dawn's light. 'That's about as close to giving up as I've ever been.'

'Somewhere back out there Whitman and whoever might still be with him could be coming on. If he is, it won't do him any good now.'

'That desert might have ate them up by now. It damned near did us. Right now we have to find a stable for these horses, and get something in our bellies too, but there's no one out here on the street. Where is everyone?'

Cort looked farther up the dirt street pointing to the lone figure of a man wearing a wide sombrero, walking toward them. 'Here comes someone. Maybe we'll get some answers.'

The man stopped, curiously looking up at the riders, tipping his hat, but said nothing. Their dusty, whiskered faces and rib thin horses told him the gringos must have crossed the desert to get here.

'Hello,' Cort tried a greeting. 'Can you tell me if we're in Mexico or not?'

The man held up both hands shaking his head. '*No comprendo, señor.*'

Cort grimaced, turning to Red. 'You know any Mexican? I sure don't.'

'Not hardly, maybe just a word or two.'

'Give it a try. We've got to find out something.'

Red lifted his arm pointing outside of town to the north.

'United States,' he said slowly, before pointing down at the ground. 'Mexico?'

'Ah, *sí*, Mexico!' The man smiled nodding his head vigorously.

'Looks like we made it across the border, all right. But we still need to talk to someone who can understand English. Let me think a minute on what else I can ask.' Red pushed his hat back on his head searching for another word that might connect. 'OK, I got one.' He looked down at his newfound friend carefully mouthing the word. '*Alcalde*?' he asked.

'*Sí*.' the man pointed up the street to a large stone building.

'*Gracias*,' Red thanked him.

'What did you say?' Cort questioned.

'I asked him if this town had a mayor. He says yes, in that building up the street. Let's get up there and see if he's right.'

'*Adios*.' Red tipped his hat before the brothers urged their horses farther down the dirt street.

The Kellers spent the next hour sitting on the building's steps waiting for someone to show up, idly glancing up and down the street until Cort finally broke the monotony. 'Not much goes around here, wherever here is.'

'No, it sure don't, but maybe it's best there isn't. After what we've had to ride through nothing don't sound too bad. Hey, wait a minute. Here comes someone,' Red pointed.

Angelo Azuar rode closer sitting astride a skinny donkey with oversized ears. He wore a large sombrero with a shock of snow white hair cascading down his temples and a large, bushy mustache to match. Pulling to a stop in front of the building he slid off the little animal tying it off to a hitching post, eyeing the *Americanos* as he did so. His rotund middle was kept in check by a wide, red sash tied at the waist. His bare feet were shod in leather sandals. One look was all Azuar needed to see his two guests were drawn thin and so were their horses.

'Good morning, amigos,' he greeted the brothers coming up. 'I am surprised to have guests this early in the morning.'

'We're just glad we found someone who can speak English,' Cort extended his hand. 'We weren't sure we would.'

'Let us go inside. The sol will be getting higher, and heat will soon follow. I don't see many *Americanos*, here. The desert keeps them to the north. You look like you found out why, no?'

Inside the mayor's office the brothers dropped into leather chairs. Cort was first to speak. 'Where exactly are we? We're not that sure yet.'

'You are in Puerto Palomas de Villa. Your people across the border simply call it Palomas. You didn't know you were in Mexico?'

'There was nothing to tell us that. No sign, no fence. We've been riding for two weeks, almost out of food and short on water. The heat is pretty bad on men and horses too.'

'*Sí*. That is the way of the desert. Can I ask what brings you on such a dangerous journey here to Palomas?'

The brothers traded quick glances, Red nodding for Cort to answer. 'We . . . ah . . . had some Indian trouble in New Mexico Territory,' he tried to sound convincing. 'They chased us south, and we thought if we could cross the border, maybe they wouldn't follow us across the desert too.'

'Apaches?' Azuar asked, already suspecting the story could not be the truth.

144

'Yes, Apaches. Once they come after you, you either have to outride them, or take on the whole Apache Nation. My brother and I didn't stand a chance against them, so we took to the desert hoping we could make it across.'

'We sometimes see a few Apaches here, but not many. As you two learned, the desert keeps most of them *al norte*. What few do come to trade for flour and sometimes cloth. They also want guns, but we have very few here. Most are owned by peasants or farmers, just old shotguns and pistols. Do you plan on staying with us long?'

'We don't know yet,' Cort answered, and this time he was telling the truth. 'We'll just have to see how things work out over the next week or maybe two. Then we can decide.'

The *alcalde* pondered Cort's words for a moment. He was curious about these two *gringos* and began forming an idea to see if he could learn more about them. He leaned forward with a suggestion and offer. 'I have a little ranchero just outside of town. I also keep a few *vaqueros* there to tend my *vacunos*, or what your people call cattle.'

'Cattle, out here?' Red interrupted.

'*Sí*, not all this land is like what you and your brother rode across. South of here there is enough well water and brush to feed my animals. I also have what you call a bunkhouse, for my men to stay in. If you would like to be my guests while you make up your mind what you will do, you can stay there. What do you say to this?'

The Kellers looked at each other in amazement. Azuar's gracious offer caught them completely by surprise. It took a moment before Cort could respond. 'That's mighty nice of you. We don't even know your name to say thanks.'

'I am called Angelo Azuar, *amigos*. And you?'

'I'm Cort Keller, and this is my brother Red. We'd both like to take you up on your offer. We've have no place else to go or stay. It would help us a lot.'

'Then it is settled. I'll take you out there now, then come back to Palomas. Let us go.'

Four days later far north from Palomas, at the beginning of the desert flats, Captain Longstreet, his line of tired cavalrymen and Marshal Whitman, pulled to a halt staring across endless miles of rock and sand ahead dancing in waves of noon day heat. A short distance in front Little Hawk also reined to a stop, his eyes studying the ground squinting against the glare. After a moment he pulled his horse around back to the line of men.

'Well, are we still on them?' Whitman demanded.

'They start across here,' the Crow tracker pointed over his shoulder.

'How long ago, can you tell?' the captain cut in.

'Maybe . . . four-five days ago.'

'That's nearly a week, if he's right,' the alarm in Longstreet's voice was obvious. 'You told me back on Mongollon, they were only hours ahead of us. How did they get a week out front!'

'There's only two of them,' Whitman quickly spoke up. 'They can ride faster and don't have to stop as often as we do. They don't have fifteen horses and men to take care of. If they went out into this desert like Little Hawk says they did, we have to continue after them. There's no other choice after coming this far.'

'Oh, yes there is, Marshal,' Longstreet countered. 'Even you admit you don't really know exactly where the border is, and I certainly don't either. For all we know we could be crossing it right here or at least not very far out there. I cannot provoke an international incident taking United States military men into Mexico, for any reason. And certainly not to run down a couple of robbers and murderers. On the American side of the border is one thing. Crossing into Mexico, is quite another.'

'Have you forgotten these two men robbed your own government pay wagon, and shot down two troopers after that?'

'No, I'm not. But I'm not going any further putting my reputation and career on the line when we have virtually no chance of closing in on them for a week or more, as you said we would. I've taken my men as far as I'm going to. If you want to continue on into who knows where, you'll have to go without me. I'll also tell you that your insane drive to kill these two men has turned this entire trip into your own personal vendetta. It even goes beyond your duty to your badge. You've made it an obsession, and a dangerous one for all involved. I'd suggest you follow me and my men back to Fort Jackson, where you can rest, regroup and get fresh supplies and horses, if you insist on continuing. For my part I'm done with it.'

Whitman's face turned red with rage. No one had ever talked to him like that. If Longstreet had been any other man than a military officer, he would have instantly gun whipped him to the ground, or worse. Instead he leaned nose to nose with the captain, his words spit out through clenched teeth.

'I know a coward when I see one, and that's what I'm looking at right now. You take your men and run for home. I don't need you to finish off the Kellers. Go on, get out of here!'

Longstreet saw the insanity in Whitman's eyes. He did not answer. It was hopeless to try. He turned away mounting his horse without a look back, shouting orders as the line of cavalrymen began moving away while the marshal and Little Hawk watched them go. As the figures grew smaller in distance, Whitman turned to the Crow tracker.

'We have enough food and water to take that on?' he

nodded out toward sandy mesquite flats shimmering in waves of heat.

Little Hawk nodded. 'Maybe four days water – two days food.'

'Then we'd better get to it.' The marshal turned for his horse without uttering another word.

Outside of Paloma, Cort and his brother sat in shade under a rickety porch in front of the bunkhouse at the Azuar *ranchero* watching several Mexican cowboys mount horses riding out for an afternoon checking on cattle. As the last *vaqueros* rode out of sight, Red got to his feet walking a few steps to lean on one of the porch uprights, thinking out loud.

'We've only been here a little more than a week, and I still can't get used to being in Mexico doing this. Know what I mean?'

'I guess I do. It is different from anyplace we've ever been, but a whole lot better than being on the run across the border wondering if you're going to catch a bullet in your back when you least expect it.'

Red snorted, a grim smile playing across his face. 'Yeah, I can't argue about that. But somehow having to leave our own country to do so still seems strange to me. Azuar is a decent enough man to take us in like he did. I just have to wonder if we'll ever be able to go back home? I've been thinking a lot about Tennessee since we got here. Mom, Dad, our old place and the whole family, or whatever is left of them these days. Maybe instead of crossing the border, we should have rode east trying to get back there?'

'You remember how things were when we left, don't you? The blue coats were looking for us, half the country was on fire, the family scattered to who knows where. I think for right now we'd better stay right here. Maybe at some point we might be able to change that, but not now. It's a little late for either you or me to start getting homesick. Let's take it easy while we can and live a little for once. We still have plenty of money, and I've been looking at how Azuar makes a living raising cattle. Maybe we could think about doing something like that.'

'I don't know much about cattle, but being that you brought up money, I sure haven't forgotten about how much we left in the bank back in Whiskeytown. How are we going to get that back and when?'

'I haven't either. At least it's not going anyplace. The bank is still the safest place for it. We'll get it back one way or the other. Don't you worry yourself about that. Try to relax a little and enjoy what we've got right here. Azuar saved our necks. Let's enjoy it while we can.'

CHAPTER THIRTEEN

'*Alcalda*, come quick,' a young boy ran into Azuar's office, eyes wide with excitement. 'Two *gringos* are riding into town, and one wears a silver badge from *Estados Unidos*!'

The mayor came to his feet instantly knowing whoever the two *Americanos* were, they were somehow connected to the Keller brothers he'd invited to stay out at his ranchero. The sudden appearance of four *Americanos* in as many weeks could not be coincidence. He followed the excited youngster outside where he pointed up the dirt street toward Nate Whitman and Little Hawk slowly riding closer. Even before they reined to a halt, Azuar could see the big man's sunburnt face was a mask of grim determination, his clothes soaked dark with dust and sweat. Beside him his dark-skinned *amigo* wore a wide brimmed hat pulled so low across his eyes, it hid any features of his face. Coming to a halt in front of the big, stone building, the mayor held up a hand of greeting. Before he could speak, Whitman did.

'Water . . . we need water.' He rubbed his stubbled face with both hands trying to beat back exhaustion. 'You speak any English?'

'*Sí*, I do *señor*. You and your *amigo* look like you should both get down and rest a while.' He turned to the youngster next to him ordering him to run inside his office to retrieve

150

the pitcher of water he kept on his desk. 'Even your *caballos* look worn out as you do. You must have come across the *desierto*, no?'

The marshal didn't answer, painfully easing himself down, grabbing the saddle horn steadying himself on shaky legs. The boy returned with the water, handing it to Whitman who gulped it down straight from the pitcher ignoring the cup. As he drank the life saving liquid, Azuar noticed his Crow sidekick uttered not one word staring straight ahead with dark eyes ignoring his own burning thirst waiting patiently for the big man to quench his thirst first. Whitman drank the entire pitcher, handing it back to the mayor who ordered the lad to run back inside to refill it.

'I've come . . . here looking for two men,' the marshal tried to catch his breath, wiping his mouth with his shirt sleeve. 'They're called the Keller brothers. The leader is named Cort. The other one is his brother, Red. We tracked them across the desert to here. You or someone around here must have seen them come through – I've got warrants on both of them – or not?'

Azuar didn't answer for several moments. He knew anything he said could lead these two to his new friends at his ranchero. Instead, he came back with a question of his own biding his time.

'What did these *Americanos* you called Kellers, do to bring you so far here to Palomas?'

'They're murderers, robbers and Johnny Rebs, who think the Civil War is still being fought. They're wild animals, and I mean to put an end to both of them either across the border back home, or here in Mexico. Have you seen them or not?'

'No, I know of no one like you describe. All I can do is ask others if they do.' The mayor stalled for more time. 'I

151

will let you know if someone else did.'

'I'll only stay here long enough to get some answers. If they're still on the run, I'll leave and continue after them. I don't care how far into Mexico they go.'

'I must ask you something,' Azuar delicately phrased his next question.

'What is it?' Whitman got to his feet while Little Hawk took his turn drinking from the pitcher.

'You wear a silver badge from your country, no?'

'I do. What about it?'

'But you are no longer in your country. Now you are here in Mexico. Your badge means little here.'

'I don't worry about that in some town like this. I still mean to run those two down and finish them off.' He reached down pulling up his six-gun. 'This is all the badge I need wherever I go.'

Azuar saw the smoldering hate in the marshal's eyes before trying to change the subject. 'I will ask if anyone knows of the men you seek. Where will you stay if I have an answer?'

'I don't imagine a place this small has a hotel, do you?'

'No, we do not. But my friend named Manuel Gonzales sometimes rents a small shack behind his house. You could try there.'

Whitman nodded with another order. 'You find out real quick. I don't want to stay here any longer than I have to. Now how do I get to this friend of yours?'

After giving directions, the marshal and Little Hawk saddled up riding slowly down the street following directions the mayor had given them. The moment they went out of sight turning off at the first corner, Azuar called out to the water boy.

'Diego, bring my burro around back of the building and hurry. I must leave town for a little while.'

Cort and Red were sitting in the bunkhouse at the ranchero, counting money they emptied out of saddle-bags, when Azuar suddenly pushed through the door, his face glistening with sweat from the hurried ride. The brothers quickly noticed the concern on his face as he came across the room.

'*Amigos*, I am afraid I have some bad news for you both.'

'We're used to it,' Cort half kidded. 'What is it, Angelo?'

'Two *Americanos* came from out of the *desietero*, as you did. One wears a silver badge. The other is Indian, but not of Mexico. He must come from *el norte*, too. The big man says he comes to find you and your brother. He has the cold steel eyes of an *hombre* who means to kill you.'

Cort looked at Red, both men instantly understanding what would come next, and what they had to do. 'Is he staying in town,' Cort questioned, 'or only riding through?'

'I think he will stay only a little while before he rides further into Mexico, if he does not find you here.'

'No, he won't have to do that. Red and I will end this right here. We're done running. Whitman's badge means nothing on this side of the border, and he knows it. Now it's just him against us. We'll settle this once and for all. Are you willing to ride back to town and tell him my brother and I will be coming in tomorrow morning?'

'*Sí*, if you wish me to.'

'I do. And tell everyone you know in town to stay off the street tomorrow. This is between him and us. I don't want anyone else hurt because of it.'

Azuar nodded half heartedly, with another idea. 'I can also tell him you are no longer here and have already left? Maybe he will leave, if I do so?'

'No, don't. You tell him exactly what I said. We'll be in early in the morning.'

The *alcalde* walked up to both men putting a hand on

153

each one's shoulder. 'I knew you came here to Palomas to leave some kind of trouble behind. Now I know what it was. I don't think this *Americano* who wears a badge is worthy of it. He seems only someone with revenge in his heart. I will pray God shields both of you tomorrow.'

'That might help Angelo, but I'll still use what I'm best at.' Cort's hand dropped down to his gun belt, gripping the handle of his six-gun.

In the dark before dawn the Kellers were up and dressed, sipping a cup of hot, strong Mexican coffee, while cleaning and checking their six-guns, each cylinder loaded with deadly, grey tipped bullets. Several *vaqueros* sat on the edge of their bunks watching the brothers, without saying a word. Sliding the wheel guns back in holsters, the brothers came to their feet strapping on gun belts.

'What about our money?' Red questioned, pointing at the saddle-bags.

'We'll leave it here. We'll both be back for it,' Cort predicted. 'It's starting to get light. Time for us to go.'

They started for the door when one of the vaqueros finally spoke up. '*Vaya con Dios, amigos.*' His face flashed a thin smile. Red understood it was not only a heartfelt goodbye, but a wish for success too.

'*Gracias.*' He nodded before exiting the room closing the door behind him.

The long ride into town saw the sky begin to brighten, the chill of desert night still crisp in the air before the fiery disk of a new sun rose to begin another day of blistering heat. Neither man uttered a word, each with his own thoughts about what was to come. After all the months, miles and hardships they'd endured riding south, it would all end in a face to face showdown lasting only seconds. Fate had predicted it from the start. It could end no other way.

Reaching Palomas, the pair reined to a halt in front of the *alcalde*'s office, easing out of the saddle. The single dirt street stood empty, low adobe buildings lining it dark and shuttered, as Cort had asked Azuar to do. Red adjusted his gun belt.

'You ready?' he asked.

'Yeah, I am. I've been ready for this a long time. Let's finish it here and now.'

They walked out into the middle of the street starting slowly toward the center of town. Reaching the first store fronts, the figures of two other men turned a corner a block away coming into view. Nate Whitman was on the left, Little Hawk next to him as they began closing the distance, before Red whispered to his brother.

'I'll take the Indian. He'll make the first move to try and give Whitman an edge.'

'Got it,' Cort answered. 'Step away from me a little further so we're not one target.'

The four men closed until barely twenty yards separated them before Whitman stopped, calling out. 'You two murderers can throw down those guns and come back across the border with me in cuffs, to face trail, or I'll kill you right where you stand. Makes no damn difference to me. Either way you're dead men!'

'We're not going anywhere,' Cort challenged. 'You and your bloody badge have come a long ways for the last time. You're all used for excuses to murder people hiding behind that tin star.'

Little Hawk instantly went for his pistol as Red predicted. In the next five seconds four bucking six-guns spit smoke, fire and lead thunder, filling the morning air with blue clouds of gun smoke. Red and Little Hawk sank to the ground, both hit by each other. Whitman tried to stand but slowly crumpled to the ground still gripping his pistols firing another wild shot into the air, before rolling over face down in the dirt. Cort, hit in the shoulder and hip, went down on one knee struggling to reach Red lying on his back gasping for air. Dark red blossoms spreading on his shirt made it clear Little Hawk had not missed either. Cort pulled himself over the top of him as Red reached up with one hand.

'Did . . . I . . . get him?'

'You did. And I finished off Whitman too. Lay still while I try to get you some help.' He started to rise.

'No . . . don't leave me alone. I'm shot up bad. Help isn't going to do me . . . any good. I want to ask you something . . . while I still can.'

'There's no time for that now.'

Red's grip tightened on his arm. 'I want to know . . . if there's any way . . . I can tell the difference between . . . heaven and hell?'

Tears welled up in Cort's eyes. He gently lifted Red cradling him in his arms. He choked back an answer fighting to control himself. 'I – guess there is. You and me have lived through a lot of hell for a long time. Heaven is all that's left for both of us.'

'I never thought . . . I'd die in . . . Mexico.' Red's hand loosened, slowly falling to his side, his eyes fading to a blank stare that saw nothing more.

Cort cried out loud unashamed, holding his brother close as misery descended on him in the lonely dirt street of Palomas. A few men hidden behind locked doors, slowly stepped outside looking wide-eyed up the street at the carnage. No one spoke. They only stared, the cloud of death hanging in the air like pungent gun smoke.

Two weeks after the savage gun fight, Cort sat alone on the front porch of the bunkhouse, staring into space. His left arm was wrapped in a sling, his hip heavily bandaged by Angelo Azuar's wife, Consuela. He was alone now without Red, unsure what to do next. The Keller gang was no more. Coy, Wic, Fan and Red all met violent deaths at the hands of Nate Whitman. The rogue lawman would no longer be able to hide behind his badge for the personal vendetta he'd carried out against them and others for so long. One question had continually haunted Cort since the street fight. Had all the killing really been worth it? Had losing his friends and even his brother, evened the score? He could not come to an answer. The one thing he was sure of was he could no longer cross the border back into the United States. He would always be a wanted man there with a price on his head, hunted by both those in and out of the law willing to risk the chance to collect a big reward money.

Over the following weeks Cort slowly recuperated from the bullet wounds, while enquiries went out up north across the southwest asking the whereabouts of a US Marshal and his Blackfoot partner. They always came back unanswered. Captain Milford Darwin Longstreet was the last man to see Whitman alive before he insisted on crossing the desert border into Mexico. He carefully noted that in his reports to superiors back at Fort Jackson. Beyond that nothing was known or heard of the two men. Eventually even those questions fell silent.

Outside of Palomas, in the rock and cactus strewn cemetery three mounds of gravelly dirt marked the recent graves of three *gringos*. Only one had a rough chiseled stone cross with a single inscription written across it. It read, 'Rest easy, my brother. You've earned your trip to eternity. We'll meet again in Glory.' The other two graves were unmarked and unkempt.

A full year after the shoot-out in town, a strange event

occurred far to the north in Whiskeytown, at the Mesalands Bank and Trust. A lone gunman described as walking with a slight limp, robbed the bank one morning soon after it opened. The robber wore a wide Mexican sombrero pulled low with a colorful *serape* over his shoulders, the features of his darkly tanned face hidden behind a red bandana. Even more puzzling was what he didn't take from the open vault. Instead of cleaning out all the trays of gold and silver coins, he took only an odd amount of money. After the robbery the bank manager poured over records that showed the stolen money added up exactly to the penny of three accounts long dormant. The names on those three accounts were John Morgan, Joe Brown and Dade Wilson. A quickly gathered posse sent out to capture the 'Mexican' bandit straggled back to town empty handed two days later saying they lost the tracks in wild country that headed due south.

Several years after the perplexing robbery, a vague word would sometimes filter back across the border about an unnamed *gringo* living many miles south of Palomas. It was said he was growing a large herd of long-horned cattle while building a beautiful *ranchero*. He'd married a young Mexican woman and she was carrying their first child. Each year, always at the same time, the *Americano* would suddenly leave the *ranchero* to disappear for two weeks. He told no one where he went, not even his wife. But the people living in Palomas began to notice a fresh bouquet of bright red flowers in a colorful clay vase adorning the stone cross during that same week each year. Cort Keller was honoring a pledge he'd made to himself and his brother. It was a ritual he would follow throughout his lifetime. Only one other man alive did know who the mysterious flower man must be. Ageing Angleo Azuar, long since retired as *alcalde* of Palomas, would keep that secret all his lifetime too. Only desert winds and silver winged vultures circling high in the hot Mexican sky, saw the lone rider place the flowers before vanishing again to ride south into obscurity and the only safety he would ever know. Señor Keller was done with the gun fights, vengeance and bloodshed he'd lived so long with. He'd begun a completely new life, in a new land, hoping what was left of his life could be lived in peace.